Mackenzie Daniel

Elsie's Married Life

A tale. Vol. 1

Mackenzie Daniel

Elsie's Married Life
A tale. Vol. 1

ISBN/EAN: 9783337344696

Printed in Europe, USA, Canada, Australia, Japan

Cover: Foto ©Andreas Hilbeck / pixelio.de

More available books at **www.hansebooks.com**

ELSIE'S MARRIED LIFE.

A TALE.

IN THREE VOLUMES.

BY

MRS. MACKENZIE DANIEL,

Author of "My Sister Minnie," "After Long Years," "Our
Brother Paul," "The Old Maid of the Family,"
"Reaping the Whirlwind," &c.

VOL. I.

London:

T. CAUTLEY NEWBY, PUBLISHER,
30, WELBECK STREET, CAVENDISH SQUARE.
1865.

ELSIE'S MARRIED LIFE.

CHAPTER I.

THE ENTERTAINERS.

It was a picture that an artist studying from nature would have delighted to paint; only I am afraid if he happened to be young, and an enthusiast, as so many young artists are, on the subject of female loveliness, he would have forgotten all about his copy in the rare pleasure of gazing at the sweet original—the human original —for there were two figures in the group I am speaking of, a girl and a dog.

The girl had light brown, waving hair, and a
Hebe face, by no means a perfect face as to out-
line, but so rich in colouring, so infinitely winning
and attractive in expression, that it was impossible to look at her once, without earnestly
desiring to look again. She was seated in childish
fashion on the floor of a handsomely furnished
drawing-room, one arm thrown round the dog,—a
huge monster, remarkable for nothing but his
size and gracelessness,—the other resting on an
ottoman, and supporting her own fair head,
which was bent over the pages of a large book,
whose leaves kept fluttering noisily, and giving
some trouble to the reader, from the occasional
gusts of summer wind, strong, sweet, and flower-
laden, that entered at the open windows.

"It won't do, Hector," she said presently,
shutting the book and tossing it from her. "The
wind is opposed to my mental improvement to-
day, that is certain. Brother Felix—your uncle,
you know, Hector—must be content to find me
no wiser than I was yesterday, concerning his

favourite Macaulay's views of the Puritans and the Cavaliers. I don't care for history, Hector; that is the solemn and, I dare say, deplorable truth; but I want to be wise about some other matters, nevertheless. And first of all, you dear hideous old Hector! I wish you could tell me why this Brother Felix, whose name stands for happiness, should be the most unhappy person in the world."

Hector replied to this appeal by lifting, very lazily, one of his shaggy paws, and placing it in the hand of his young mistress. The act might have been suggestive, but it was scarcely enlightening, and the young mistress only shook her head and kissed her faithful companion, as the door opened, and a gentleman dressed in black, and with a fine though rather stern face, stood upon the threshhold.

"Only you, Elsie?" he said, advancing a few paces and looking round the room. "Where are all the others?"

"Some out, I believe, some dressing," returned

Elsie, yawning a little wearily, as she rose with evident reluctance from her comfortable position beside Hector, who yawned too, and stretched himself in most ungraceful fashion, as his quietude was thus disturbed. "And unless you have come home earlier than usual, Felix, it is high time that I was dressing too. There is company to-day, you know."

"Oh yes, I know, indeed," said the gentleman, discontentedly, "and I would have given a good deal to have got out of making one of the party, only my mother put it in the light of a favour to herself. I remember old Mr. Carlyon when I was a boy, and I never liked him then. I am sure I shall like his son still less."

"Now, Felix, I do call that very prejudiced and disagreeable of you," exclaimed Elsie, going up to her brother—he looked quite fifteen years older than herself—and laying her pretty little hand caressingly on his arm. "I have heard you say it is wrong to judge people before we thoroughly know them. What is it, then, to judge them before we have even seen them ? Tell me that, please; or shall 1 ask Hector ? "

" It is not judging him, Elsie, to say I am sure *I* shall dislike him," returned Felix, in a milder tone, as he glanced down at the small, slight winning-looking creature standing beside him.· " He may be a hero or a saint, and yet fail to please such a churlish, unsympathising, cold-hearted fellow as myself, eh, Elsie ? "

" Well, but Felix, you know I don't believe you to be any of these things," said Elsie earnestly, though her bright face assumed for a moment the same puzzled, enquiring look it had worn when she was talking to her dog. " And why you want the world at large to think badly of you I cannot imagine. I know you are not happy——"

" Child, child," interrupted her brother quickly, and with a tone of authority, " you know nothing ; and guessing is an unprofitable occupation for little girls. Go and put on your furbelows and trinkets, Elsie, since this introduction *must* take place, and, if Joanna is ready, ask her to come down here to me; I want to talk to her before these people arrive."

In less than ten minutes after Elsie had closed the drawing-room door, it opened again, and admitted another sister of the handsome, gloomy-visaged man, who stood with his arm leaning on the marble mantelpiece waiting for her.

"I thought," he said, glancing down slightly at the over-plain, almost quaker-like costume of the new comer, "that I might reckon on *your* not requiring an extra half hour to adorn yourself for these Carlyons, and I wanted to speak to you privately about Elsie."

"About Elsie?" repeated the very quiet personage he addressed, in a voice so measured, and apparently unsympathizing, that any one less accustomed to it than the members of her own family, would have been utterly discouraged from proceeding.

"Yes," resumed Felix, as the sister he had summoned came and stood on the hearth-rug be-

side him. "I want to tell you that I feel certain.
the meeting of this evening has special reference
to her. Old Carlyon would not have proposed
introducing his son here without an object. My
father would not have acceeded to it without an
object. They both, unhappily, consider money the
only thing worth living for. Edgar Carlyon will
be one of the richest commoners in England, and
our poor little Elsie, if she lives to be twenty,
comes in for the greater part of her godmother's
fortune. The fathers have put their heads together, and resolved that the children shall
fall in love with each other. It is for this that
Edgar has been recalled from abroad. He is
more than half a foreigner, you know, and hates
England. If Elsie had remained the invalid she
has been for the last four years, we should have
heard nothing of this young man. Heaven knows
I have rejoiced with you all in her marvellous and
unhoped for restoration to health; but if it is to
bring about a nearer connection with that family,
if it is to make her, child as she is, the wife of a

Carlyon, I would rather have followed her to her grave."

He spoke these last words excitedly, almost passionately, and Joanna, whose face had never altered its calm expression the whole time, replied rebukingly —

"You have no right to say or to feel that, Felix, though I should quite agree with you in deploring a marriage between Elsie and a young man whose long residence abroad has no doubt given him unsettled principles, and at any rate must have hindered the growth of the most ordinary religious sentiments. But if our elders are really bent upon bringing about such an union, neither your interference nor mine will be of the slightest avail."

"I know that, Joanna" (this was spoken bitterly); "but I thought you might do something with Elsie herself. If she should not be fascinated with this fellow—I have been told he is both handsome and accomplished—I am not afraid that they will compel her to marry him.

Elsie, with all her gentleness, has a pretty strong will of her own, and she is too great a favorite with everybody at home for there to be much fear of this will being thwarted—they will all try to influence her no doubt, and what I want is to get your influence exerted on the other side. Do you understand now?"

" Not quite. It may be that, from circumstances, I am just a little more to Elsie than her other sisters, but you must be aware, Felix, that however much I may be to her it would all count for nothing if she should give away her heart—and how am I to prevent this?"

The question was to the point, and the gentleman certainly looked puzzled for a minute or so. Then he said (and this seemed rather wide of the mark)—

" Joanna, I have fancied for some time that you would like nearly as well as I should to see our little Elsie the wife of James Oliver. He loves her with an honest, manly, love; and if any marriage in the world could be a happy one, these two, in coming together, would be secure of happiness."

While Felix thus warmly spoke, something fainter and more transient than a blush, had dawned and disappeared on the pale cheek of his attentive listener. It was quite unobserved, however, by her brother, who, intent on his own thoughts and purpose, waited eagerly for her answer.

Very slowly, clearly, and deliberately it came at last, as if every word had been carefully weighed in the balance of prudence or conscience.

"I did not know that Mr. Oliver's attachment to Elsie was a certain or acknowledged fact. If it is so, and she could like him sufficiently in return, there is no one to whom I could so confidently entrust her."

"I was right then in supposing you would be on our side," rejoined Felix in a tone of greater satisfaction than any in which he had hitherto spoken, "and surely, when Elsie knows that Oliver loves her, she will feel as we do that there

is scarcely a man in the world to be compared
to him. He is diffident and distrustful of his
powers of charming women—good, noble-minded
men always are so—and then he has unfortunately
heard of this money coming to Elsie; and so
he would sooner die than speak of his attachment
to her. But you see if I could give him the
smallest hope that she cared for him, the whole
affair would be easy enough.   I don't like to
sound her myself—men are clumsy in these delicate
matters; but you, Joanna, are the very one to
do it excellently.   I can trust it wholly to you;
and above all, don't delay it—don't let this new
man succeed in making any way with her before
you have interested her heart on behalf of poor
Oliver. Of course there is no time to speak before
the meeting of to-day, but in a single interview
the boldest fellow in the world couldn't do much ;
and perhaps, when you go to bed to-night, you
may manage something."

"I will at least try," said Joanna; and then
Felix looking at his watch declared he had only

ten minutes to prepare for dinner, and hastening out of the room he left his quiet sister standing alone in the spot where she had first joined him, and from which she had not stirred when, in another five or six minutes, two new ladies—members of the same family, and accompanied by a little boy of about four years old, magnificently attired—came noisily into the drawing-room, and arranged their ample and flowing skirts, with an eye to graceful effect, upon the largest of the damask couches.

The elder of these, Mrs. Paget, was the mother of the family now introduced—a stout, well preserved matron of about fifty-five, but unlike stout matrons in general, especially when well-preserved, her countenance had a restless, peevish look in it, which was anything but agreeable to see. She gave one the idea of a person who was intensely anxious concerning the impression she might make on those around her, intensely anxious that her importance, either as a lady of fashion or the head of a fine family, or something of which she was severely conscious herself, should be recognised by all with whom she was brought in contact. Her toilet on the present occasion was rich and elaborate, and she looked down at it from time to time admiringly, frowning darkly at the little boy if he ventured to approach near enough to crumple any of the silken folds she had taken such pains to arrange carefully.

The lady who had entered the room with Mrs. Paget was attired in widow's weeds, but her dress was also as elegant and expensive as was in any way consistent with the continued state of mourning her white muslin cap and broad streamers suggested. She was a good-looking woman of about thirty ; but on her face too might be discovered—though in general it was better concealed—an expression of discontent and uneasiness as if she had fallen out of love with life, and was seeking vainly for some new object to occupy the void in her affections.

This was Mrs. Vining (the eldest daughter of

the House of Paget), who in the short space of one year had married a supposed rich man, and been returned, a penniless widow, to the bosom of her own disappointed family. It was a most uncomfortable position for any woman—a proud one especially—to be placed in, and Georgina Vining had some excuse for her habitual ill-temper and fretfulness; but, unfortunately, ill-temper and fretfulness never make 'any position better, rather the reverse; and it was a bad example to set to her little boy, now getting on to childhood's most observant age, and who, sometimes extravagantly petted, sometimes unjustly snarled at both by grandmamma and mamma, threatened to become one of the most unruly and odious boys in the world. He was a very pretty child; and dressed now in a blue velvet tunic and falling lace collar, he looked quite a little picture, and his mother was inclined in consequence to be very gracious and indulgent to him.

"Come to me, my beauty," she said, when

grandmamma had for the second or third time showed manifest symptoms of not coveting his too near proximity to her silk dress. " I am not afraid of being hurt by those pretty little hands—they are clean as pinks, aren't they, my darling? and Arthur is going to be the best of boys to-day, and to let the gentlemen see how well he can behave—Joanna," looking up suddenly, and addressing her sister, " he may sit by you at dinner this evening if you like. You never wear anything that will spoil, even if he should, pretty lamb! spill his gravy or anything over you. I, who am so poor, living in fact on charity, must take care of the few company dresses I possess."

" Arthur can sit by me, if you wish it," said Joanna, without any appearance, however, of esteeming the arrangement an especial privilege; " but I should be as unwilling to have my dress spoiled as you can be. I consider myself responsible for every penny I spend."

"Oh, humbug!" retorted Georgina, rudely. "That doesn't go down with me, you know. But take care of the child to-day, in any case, and if he hurts that old grey silk, I will manage somehow to give you another."

"I think, my dear," put in Mrs. Paget now, glancing through her jewelled eye glass at her second daughter, "I think you might have dressed yourself rather more becomingly, in honour of the friends we are expecting to-day. That grey silk *is* old, Joanna, and your brother gave you a very handsome Indian muslin some time ago."

"But it is not made up yet, mamma," the girl replied, a little wearily, "and the silk I have on is perfectly clean and well preserved. I don't suppose either Mr. Carlyon or his son will have any eyes for me."

"Probably not," observed the mother, complacently, as her restless glance travelled round to the door. "What a time that little puss Elsie is before she comes down; but I suppose Carter is bent upon turning her out something prodigious to-day."

"Labour lost in Elsie's case, for she *must* look beautiful and bewitching in anything," said Mrs. Vining, adding immediately, "Ought not poor Lillie to have been here by this time?"

"Poor Lillie!" repeated the mother with a sigh that was more fretful than sorrowful, "May be he won't let her come, after all."

"How I should enjoy having the punching of that man's head," remarked Georgina Vining, in a savage accent, "and if I were in poor Lillie's place, I would do it, too, twenty times a day at least. Oh, here's somebody coming. Arty, darling, run away from the door, or you'll be knocked down."

It was only Elsie who entered now, dressed as simply and becomingly as possible, in a white flowing dress of Indian muslin, and with some pretty pale blue flowers, just gathered from the conservatory, showing amidst the rich masses of her bright brown hair.

Mrs. Paget's face relaxed into a smile, quite a cheerful pleasant smile, as her youngest daughter came and stood before her, asking laughingly if she was fine enough for the fine people who were expected. Mrs. Vining stretched out one arm, and drew the sweet face down to her own to be kissed, and Joanna, moving for the first time since Felix had left the room, came quietly to Elsie's side, and gave a little tender squeeze to the hand her sister immediately extended to her.

Whatever else this somewhat quarrelsome family might find to dispute and differ about, they were all perfectly agreed in loving and spoiling Elsie.

The next time the door opened it admitted Mr. Paget, a tall, stout man of about sixty, who looked round complacently on the group assembled and said he thought they would all " do," but it was getting late, and why had not poor Lillie arrived.

Mrs. Vining's immediate accession of colour suggested that she was about to offer some further observations on the relief it would afford her to have " that man's " head punched, when the grave, sad face of Felix Paget appeared in the doorway.

" Poor Lillie has just come," he said ; " she is getting out of her cab.   Perhaps one of you girls would like to go upstairs with her."

CHAPTER II.

THE GUESTS.

A FEW words, while "poor Lillie" is receiving her welcome, concerning the guests for whose honorable entertainment so much ado was being made in the Paget family.

Mr. Carlyon, the elder, had been many years ago partner with Mr. Paget, in one of the largest and wealthiest mercantile houses in London. When it was judged expedient by both of these gentlemen to establish a corresponding house in Paris, Mr. Carlyon had gone with his family to reside in that city, and very soon after he had decided, somewhat abruptly, upon dissolving partnership with his friend, and carrying on the foreign business alone. From that time nothing had prospered with Mr. Paget, while Mr. Carlyon's wealth had gone on steadily and rapidly increasing. He had lost in the interval a wife, a daughter, and two sons, and there was no one left to inherit a fortune—said to be already gigantic—but the young man Edgar Carlyon, whose name has been mentioned in the previous chapter. This young man had been educated entirely abroad, and had spent the last five years of his life in travelling through Europe, Asia, and America. He had the reputation of being rarely accomplished, and this, united to an indisputably handsome person, would have made him, even without the golden halo that surrounded him, an object of very general attraction and fascination. As it was, he might, no doubt, have chosen a wife amongst the highest and the fairest of the daughters of the land, but hitherto he had not seemed to covet such an adjunct to his many advantages—his heart was possibly a cold one—and if Mr. Carlyon, the elder, had proposed his introduction to the Pagets with any such view as that suggested by Felix to his sister Joanna, it certainly was without the slightest participation in the plot on the part of his son. The merest hint that he was desired to fall in love with any special lady would have secured for the lady, though she might have been an angel, Mr. Edgar Carlyon's very cordial dislike.

The father was perfectly aware of this little fact, so he had made out that it was a matter of business with old Paget, "something in which he might find him useful by and bye," that had dictated his wish to renew the former friendliness between the families—a friendliness that was to commence by the acceptance of their eagerly proffered hospitality of to-day.

"But it will be an awful bore, won't it?" said Mr. Carlyon, the younger, as he put the last finishing touches to his really faultless toilet before a splendid mirror in the drawing-room of one of the finest west-end hotels, while his respectable and equally well-dressed parent sat smoking a cigar on the sofa—"It will be an awful bore doing the agreeable to these cockney people—half a dozen girls, I think you said, with red arms bare to the elbow, and very low necked dresses, *à l'Anglaise*, and hair in lanky ringlets—oh, hang business, I say, if it condemns gentlemen of taste to dine, even once a year, in such company as this."

It almost appeared that the respectable parent on the sofa chuckled softly to himself as his elegant son was thus speaking, but he only said quite gravely—

"No, no, Edgar, you are drawing on your imagination, not on your memory, now. I never told you a word of six girls, or bare arms, or low necked frocks. There are only two unmarried daughters, and one of these is a bonnie lassie enough—at least she is thought so by a good many, for her portrait was in the academy this year; but I don't see much in her for my part. I never was so mad about your pink and white English beauties."

" And the other girl," asked Edgar, as he gave the final twist to his silky moustache, and then leant back to rest from his labours on a *chaise longue ;* " what is she like ? "

" Oh, like nothing at all ; " laughed the father, throwing the end of his cigar on to the balcony, " pale, washed out, insipid,—religious too, with such a vengeance that I believe the whole family are sick of it, and of her.   She was at a Moravian school in Germany, and brought these notions home with her."

" How particularly unpleasant ! " exclaimed Edgar, with a very natural shudder, " and will this misguided young person dine at table, do you think ? or do fasting and sackcloth enter into her views of Christian duty ? "

" I don't know ; " laughed the father, as of course so excellent a jest deserved to be laughed at, " but I fancy we shall have to see her with the others.   Then there is a widow, concerning whom I ought very seriously to warn you, for she will set her cap (such a cap as it is too, with strings four feet by one and a-half) at both of us. She was the eldest girl and married that fool Vining, who was once junior partner with old Paget and myself. When he left us and went into business on his own account, he did for himself, with speculations that all turned out ill, in six months. That man never had the brains of a tomtit, and when there was a rumour that he had committed suicide, I made a point of contradicting it everywhere; impossible that he could have deemed such brains as his worth powder and shot."

" Ah!" said Mr. Edgar Carlyon, by no means interested either in the brains or the fate of the departed Vining, " and that is all the family, I suppose, except the son, whom I will not trouble you to describe to me."

" No, there is yet another daughter, a married one too; but I have never seen her, and only heard her alluded to as 'poor Lillie!' I gather from the fact of her having obtained this designation that she has not drawn a prize in the matrimonial lottery. The Pagets are certainly anything but a fortunate family. The son is a doctor now, you know, and writes M.D. after his name."

"Hang him!" exclaimed Mr. Edgar, rousing a moment from his languor and indifference, "I don't care if he writes M.F. for madman and fool. I believe him to be both; and but to oblige you I would have met on terms of friendliness the Prince of Darkness himself, sooner than this Felix Paget."

"I have not seen him since he was a boy," said the father, waiving his companion's sudden excitement, "he was absent when I was in England last winter, and, as you may remember, circumstances prevented our meeting during the time he was in France five years ago. Besides that I make a point of never meddling with other people's business I have good reasons for believing—very good reasons, Edgar—that in reference to the matters you are thinking of just now, there were grave faults on the part of more than Felix Paget. Since it is likely that these people may be useful to me,—and to you, through me,—it will be our policy to let by-gones be by-gones. Seven o'clock, by jingo! and their cook is as punctual as the horse guards."

"And here is the carriage," yawned the younger gentleman as the door opened and the waiter entered to announce that Mr. Carlyon's equipage was in waiting; "we can surely get to Bayswater in twenty minutes."

Which they did, being ushered into the presence of the expectant family just as Mrs. Paget had received a third private message from her *chef de cuisine* to the effect that another five minutes would complete the destruction of one of the neatest and most admirable dinners that was ever cooked.

CHAPTER III.

DR. PAGET'S PARTNER.

IN consequence of the extreme urgency of the case, the introductions were all hurried over somewhat indecorously, and Mr. Edgar Carlyon, before he well knew where he was, found himself leading into the dining room a tall lady in sable silk, the streamers of whose muslin head dress were blown into his face as they passed an open window in the hall, and who wound up her apology for the annoyance he was thus subjected to, by a sigh so gentle and so delicately insinuated, that any one with human feeling must have been instantly subjugated, and have resolved to console the fair widow, if that were possible, at any cost. What Mr. Edgar Carlyon resolved on was to manœuvre, on reaching the dining-room, so that he might escape sitting next to the lady now leaning on his arm. He had caught one glimpse of a face that appeared to him very radiant and very beautiful, and to be placed near the owner of that face had become his sudden, eager, passionate desire.

And fate, in the shape of Mrs. Paget, stood his friend on this occasion, for just as Georgina Vining was going to subside gracefully into the chair beside that of her handsome escort, her mother thoughtfully discovered that there was an open window at her back which would be sure to give her cold, and called on Elsie to change places with her sister.

By this arrangement the young gentleman obtained what he wanted, while the widow (not looking in the least grateful for her mamma's affectionate solicitude) was handed over to a seat between the elder Carlyon and the " poor Lillie" who has yet to be introduced to the reader.

I will only say now that this young lady was a few years older than Elsie ; that she had a bright, cheerful, even lively countenance, not wanting in prettiness, though it was less refined both in feature and expression than that of her youngest sister ; that she was the last person in the world on whom a casual observer would have bestowed an epithet of compassion as she gave one the idea of having spirits and life enough both for herself and those members of her family who were less happily gifted.

Henceforth poor Lillie shall speak for herself.

"Isn't it jolly that I have got away to-day ?' she whispered to Mrs. Vining the moment an unintelligible muttering, which passed for a thanksgiving, was concluded at the head of the table, " I had such a fight before I could manage it. Dick swore if I left the house he would horsewhip me back, but I hid away all his whips, and then dared him to stop me. I think he would though, if he hadn't had a ferocious headache which made him glad at last to get rid of me. Didn't I talk loud, and stamp about the room, and knock the furniture about, by accident? Oh, it was such fun, you can't think; and when the cab drove up to the door, he was ready to swear that if I didn't leave him he'd horsewhip me out of the house, instead of into it."

The widow, who had by no means recovered her temper, replied gloomily that one of these days she must punch that man's head for him, and then fell upon Lillie and told her that she was more than an idiot for staying with such a brute.

" Fiddlesticks !" retorted Lillie with spirit, " what should I gain by coming home again? Dick's all very well sometimes, and the other times I know how at least to keep my neck on my shoulders. If it had been Elsie now, she would have had hers twisted long ago. A gentle or a timid woman married to Dick Wilmot would find herself nowhere in three months. I say, Georgina (in a lower whisper), somebody is.

tremendously good-looking, and I do believe he's caught already."

"Hush, Lillie," rebuked the widow with an expressive frown, "and do eat your dinner like a good child, while I talk a bit to my neighbour on the right. Mamma, you see, is too busy to attend to him."

The elder Mr. Carlyon had no objection at all to be entertained by the pensive Mrs. Vining, since he saw that matters were going on quite as he wished on the opposite side of the table. Elsie's shy, low voiced answers to Mr. Edgar's amiabilities were evidently deepening the impression her fresh young loveliness and grace had made upon him. In all his wanderings in distant lands he had seen nothing that so nearly approached his standard of perfection as this type of youthful womanhood now before him. He wondered greatly at Elsie Paget, not knowing anything of the influences which had combined to render her what she was. The English girls he had occasionally met abroad had given him an unfavourable opinion of his countrywomen in general—so unfavourable, indeed, that whenever his father had spoken to him, either jestingly or seriously, on the subject of marriage, he had declared that he had rather choose a wife from any nation under the sun than from his own. Now Mr. Carlyon (*père*) though liking well enough to live in Paris, had no fancy for a Parisian daughter-in-law, and it was his dread that Edgar might be caught in the end by some French adventuress, who would scatter in a year or two the money he had spent his life in earning, that made him so anxious to secure for his son a simple, modest, and at the same time comfortably dowered English wife.

Elsie was the only one of the Paget family whom he would have selected for this distinguished honour, even had all the sisters been free and as amply provided for as she was. He did not admire Mrs. Paget in the least, nor consider her adapted in any way to the training of young daughters; but he knew (for he was a man of quick observation and keen discernment), that Elsie's long illness had removed her out of the sphere of her mother's jurisdiction, and surrounded her with an atmosphere in which her sweet ductile mind had been left free to expand according to natural laws, instead of being controlled and turned out of its healthy course by false and hollow and altogether absurd conventionalities.

Mr. Carlyon was essentially a worldly man, as well as a man of the world, but for all this, he had a very clear notion of what a woman ought to be, and he was quite sufficiently attached to his only son to desire earnestly that, if he married, he should choose a wife both fair and virtuous—one in whom her husband's heart might safely trust, and whose children might hereafter " rise up and call her blessed."

" And the thing's done!" he said to himself with singular complacency, noticing, as Lillie Wilmot had noticed, the way in which the young people were engrossed with each other.

And then he turned and began an animated dialogue that almost merged into a flirtation—so pleasantly excited he was—with the lady of the gorgeous streamers.

The whole dinner, beginning so well, went off admirably. If Dr. Felix Paget was less careful to add his quota to the entertainment of his father's guests than might have been expected of him, nobody seemed to remark it. He was nearly always silent and pre-occupied during the very few hours he spent each day with his own family, and they had all come to understand his moods, and to accept them as something which it would be beyond their power to alter. He sat to-day by his sister Joanna, and when he talked at all it was to her, or to the spoiled little fellow who had been committed to her care, and whom she found it tolerably hard to manage.

The ladies retired early to the drawing-room, Mrs. Paget thoroughly appreciating the importance of shortening a first interview between two persons mutually attracted by some outward grace or fascination which contemplated too long at a time might lose a portion of its charm. Besides, she really wanted a good hour to talk to poor Lillie, who could get from her own home so rarely, and whose domestic grievances formed an ever interesting and exciting topic of conversation in the Paget family.

So as soon as they all reached the pretty drawing-room, opening on a small but charmingly laid out garden, Mrs. Paget rang for tea to be served to them (while the gentlemen had their coffee in the dining-room) and, inviting Lillie and Elsie to a seat on either side of her, signified that Mrs. Vining and Joanna could join the coterie if they pleased.

Mrs. Vining did please, for not only was she in a much better temper than before dinner, but the anticipation of hearing of some more battles between poor Lillie and " that man " was always a temptation to her, and one which she was not in the habit of resisting. Joanna having no taste for such highly seasoned dishes—thinking indeed that her sister's trials with a coarse and low-minded husband were scarcely fit subjects for drawing-room gossip, said she would take Arthur into the garden—and even Elsie on this occasion did not ask her to change her mind.

The four ladies thus left together sipped their tea and discussed a great many matters with a great deal of spirit, while the summer twilight was gradually stealing down upon them, and one at least of their number was beginning to weary a little of this feminine gossip, and to think the party in the dining-room long in joining them.

Before they came, Joanna and Arthur entered from the garden, bringing with them another guest, whom it will be necessary to introduce formally to the reader.

Mr. James Oliver, surgeon by profession—and partner to Dr. Felix Paget! A young man of about six or seven and twenty—plain rather than handsome, fair rather than dark, tall rather than short; and yet in describing whom nobody would ever think of saying he was either plain, or fair, or tall.   Probably, by most persons, he would be described as simply gentlemanly and agreeable looking.   Let us take him at this modest estimate. By and bye we shall know more about him, and when the inner man is fully revealed we shall perhaps have grown indifferent to the outward form and expression.

Joanna merely said, as she preceded this gentleman into the room, " Mamma, here is Mr. Oliver.   He is distressed at the thought of having come too early.   Pray reassure him on this subject, since all *my* assurances go for nothing."

Then she went into a quiet corner with some work, and spoke no more.

"As if you were not always welcome," exclaimed Elsie warmly, getting up immediately and shaking hands with the new comer, while Mrs. Paget and the widow each murmured a few words of commonplace politeness—"Felix will be in directly ; but until he comes I will, if you like, play some of your favourite airs to you—and here is Hector actually making an effort to wake up, and bid you good evening. If *that* isn't a compliment 1 don't know what is. Now do speak to him, and thank him for his friendliness."

The young man stooped and patted the huge animal's shaggy head.

"Good dog, good dog," he said in a voice that was singularly sweet and noticable, but he spoke absently, and his eyes seemed mesmerically attracted to the dog's fair young mistress, who certainly looked, in the shadowy twilight, with her floating white dress and sunny hair, as pure and angelic a vision—(to give utterance to the thoughts about her that were filling just then the gazer's mind), as any daughter of Eve has ever looked since Eden became a memory and a dream.

"Yes, he is indeed a good dog, a darling dog," resumed Elsie, almost stupidly unconscious of the passionate admiration she herself was exciting —"but am I to play to you or not, Mr. Oliver? You do not appear as music mad as usual, to-night."

"Will you sing?" he said, rousing himself now, and evidently tutoring his voice that it might not betray the emotions this simple gazing at Elsie had awakened—"I should like to hear 'Fairy bells' to-night; you always sing that so feelingly."

"Nobody but you cares for such poor singing as mine," laughed Elsie, going to the piano and lighting one only of the wax candles that had been placed ready upon it—"and I assure you I should be very sorry to be detected by the gentlemen from the dining-room in mimicing or murdering 'Fairy bells,' however feelingly. But they won't be in just yet, I dare say, and you can watch and give me the first notice of their approach."

Then she sat down—he at a little distance from her—and sang very prettily and plaintively the ballad her friend had asked for; while Joanna from her dark corner watched them both, and wondered she had been blind so long, and would have bestowed a world of sympathy upon *him*,

but that she had a grief of her own so new that
—good, unselfish girl though she was—she could
not choose but give her tenderest pity to the heart
whose pain just now had become a real physical
consciousness of suffering, which she knew she
must hide evermore as jealously and carefully as
if that suffering were sin.

> " I dreamt, 'twas but a dream,
>   Thou wert my bride, love,
>   I dreamt that we were wandering
>   Side by side, love,
>   I, earth's happiest son, and thou
>   Her loveliest daughter;
>   While fairy bells came tinkling o'er the water.
>   Merrily, merrily, merrily it fell—
>   The echo of that fairy bell."

And he who listened was in a dream, too, a
dream of unimaginable sweetness and beauty;
which intoxicated all his senses, and made him
for awhile—just these few blissful minutes—forget that any obstacles could exist to the attain-
ment of his soul's most ardent desire, to the ful-

filment of the hope which, at first unknown to himself, had been slowly twining itself amongst the deepest roots of his life since the day, nearly two years ago, when Felix Paget sent him—his old schoolfellow but new partner—to see professionally his little sick sister.

Dating from that time, James Oliver had scarcely been a day without visiting Elsie, and very soon he came to be received rather as a friend than as a doctor, to be welcomed eagerly in the sick room with the flowers, or books, or sunshine of some kind he was sure to bring, and to be allowed, whenever he chose to ask for it, the privilege of reading aloud to the sisters, while Joanna (Elsie's constant nurse and companion), worked diligently and silently beside him, and Elsie listened and chatted and sometimes quarrelled, by way of a change, with this ever patient friend ; but was always sweet and winning, and grateful.

Not less sweet, or grateful, or winning when, her long illness terminated, she emerged from the shadow of that weary sick room, and took her place in the family as darling and idol of them all. But everything except Elsie had seemed to change for James Oliver from that time. Besides that he had no longer an excuse for his daily and lengthy visits, he found that Mr. and Mrs. Paget received him with much less warmth and friendliness than they had done, while their child's precarious state made it a matter of indifference that she should be exposed to the constant society of a young man who had no expectations, and whose profession was never likely to secure him more than a modest competence. Had Elsie and Mr. Oliver taken a fancy to each other under the circumstances which first authorised their constant intercourse, it would have signified very little. Had he as a doctor, chosen to burden himself with an invalid wife, that would have been his own concern, and one with which these prudent parents would not have thought of meddling. But Elsie, with recovered health and improved beauty—Elsie, the admired of all beholders, was quite another thing ; and Mr. James Oliver, however charming and amiable, must now carry his devotion, if indeed he felt any to speak of, elsewhere.

It was a pity that the gentleman himself should not at once have been able to see matters in the same reasonable light; a pity, too, that Felix Paget, esteeming this old school friend of his so highly, should have indirectly encouraged him still to hope for Elsie as the ultimate reward of his long and sincere attachment to her. These little mistakes and *contretemps* will happen in the most carefully regulated households, and in the present case they had gradually brought about the dangerous mental state in which James Oliver sat and listened, on the night I am describing, to Elsie's warbling voice, and felt as if fairy bells of the most thrilling and melodious kind were echoing their ravishing notes in every chamber of his heart.

He was far too entranced and absorbed to hear the door at the far end of the room open to admit the party from the dining-room; and it was Joanna who went up to the instrument and warned her sister of the approach of their guests, just as Elsie had sung, smiling round at her most attentive listener in pretty scorn of the sentimental words she was uttering—

"That vision past away, and thou hast left me!"

And he who understood and returned the smile suspected not that these foolish words would evermore be associated in his mind with the too truthful prophecy they embodied.

CHAPTER IV.

TOO LATE.

It is probable that the very first look that Mr. Oliver directed towards the gentleman who interrupted Elsie's singing, causing her to rise abruptly from the piano with a sudden crimson in her face, revealed to him the very shadowy nature of the paradise in which he had been revelling.

Felix Paget came up to him as he stood for a second or two lost in the contemplation either of Edgar Carlyon and Elsie, or of his own folly.

"What a suffocating evening!" Dr. Paget said, because he wanted to bring his friend out of

cloudland, and also because, under the circumstances to which he could not help being alive, he
really felt it to be suffocating, " will you come
out and have a cigar with me, while the ladies are
making up their minds how they shall amuse us.
I want to hear what you did about that dislocation
case this afternoon."

So the two went out into the garden together,
and when Felix returned, half an hour later to
the drawing-room, he explained that Mr. Oliver
had been summoned to the surgery, to attend to
several unexpected cases, and that he begged to
be excused if he was unable to make his appearance again that evening.

The surgery was close to the private residence
of Dr. Paget's family, and could be reached through
a gate which the doctor himself had caused to be
put up at the lower end of the garden.

Mrs. Vining, who was a very accomplished
musician, was at the piano when her brother again
joined the party. Old Mr. Carlyon stood near
her turning over the leaves at her bidding, as he

did not know a note of music himself; and Edgar and Elsie sat at a little table near them, looking over a picture book.

Mr. and Mrs. Paget were both trying hard to keep awake but succeeding indifferently, while Joanna and Lillie appeared to be taking it in turns to divert Master Arthur and hinder him from being a nuisance to everybody in the room.

" Why don't you send that boy to bed ?" asked Felix, who was clearly not in the best of humours, " it's quite absurd having him up at this hour of the night."

" He won't go till his mother insists on it," replied Joanna looking very weary, " and Georgina has been at the piano ever since you went out."

" Besides, I like to have him with me, dear child !" added Lillie, drawing the spoiled and somewhat reluctant little fellow into her arms, " I have nothing to love at home, Felix. You should not grudge me this small crumb of comfort when it is within my reach. For a child like Arthur—of my own—I would give—almost my soul."

" Lillie, Lillie!" said Joanna, in a voice that would have been stern if it had not been so very sad, " why will you talk so recklessly ? How do we know—any of us—what is for our good?"

" Leave the boy with her, and come over to that sofa with me," hurriedly put in the brother, as if he had no great fancy for Joanna's preaching, or felt its uselessness in the present case. " I have some directions to give you about those sick old people you have undertaken to visit."

And as Dr. Felix Paget was a strictly conscientious man, he prefaced his conversation with Joanna, the second he had held that day, by instructing her very carefully in the treatment to be observed in the cases of those very poor sick patients of his whom his sister had volunteered to look after, to the extent that her other charitable labours would permit. This done, he dismissed the whole matter abruptly, and as abruptly said—

"Joanna, I fear we shall be too late. It strikes me that Elsie is falling in love with that conceited and artificial fellow as fast as ever she can. What do you think?"

Instead of answering this question, Joanna asked with more eagerness than she wished or meant to exhibit,

"Did Mr. Oliver go away because he guessed anything, because he was hurt, or unhappy?"

"He did not confide in me if such was the case, Jo. I believe something *had* cast a sudden gloom over him; but the patients were really there. I should, however, have seen them had I thought Oliver would have enjoyed the evening here. Elsie is a little fool to be taken with the first good-looking dandy who talks nonsense to her. But I can't give it up yet, Joanna. You must do your very utmost to pull down this night's work, and recommend Oliver to her. He would make her happy—that other man would make her miserable. Besides, I feel for him, for my good, true-hearted friend who loves what he does love with the whole force of his honest nature. Edgar Carlyon would love her—perhaps while her youth and beauty lasted—not a minute beyond; and Elsie, going out from such an atmosphere of devotion as that which has ever surrounded her, would pine to death in a colder air, even should coldness be the only grievance. Joanna, you see all this as I do, I am sure, and you will do what you can, won't you?"

"And if I fail, Felix?"

She said this in a tone so suggestive of her own certainty of failure, that her brother replied almost angrily—

"I don't really believe you are half interested in the matter, Jo, or you would *determine* to succeed. I must leave you now, for I have a word to say to old Carlyon, and I see he is wearying a little of Georgina's lengthy performance. Try to give her a hint that we have had enough of it for the present, and get Lillie to sing. They won't stay much longer."

But Joanna either forgot this errand or did not

feel disposed to execute it. When Felix had finished talking with her, she quietly slipped out of the room, confident of not being missed or enquired for, and spent the remainder of the evening alone upstairs.

About eleven o'clock, when, tired of gazing out at the summer moon shining in its restful majesty in a purple sky, Joanna had just closed the window and lighted her lamp preparatory to her evening reading, Elsie (who shared the same bedroom), came in—bright, unwearied and joyous-looking, and asked her sister why she had so early deserted them all.

" I had had enough of it, darling," said Joanna kindly, if still sadly, " and I was no use there— certainly no ornament either; so I came away. Have the Carlyons been long gone ?"

" No ; not more than a quarter of an hour. Jo, dear, do you know why Mr. Oliver did not stay? do you think he has really patients waiting for him ?"

A better opening Joanna could not have desired; and though she rightly conjectured that Elsie had only named Mr. Oliver because she wanted to defer the moment in which she must speak of somebody who had interested her far more than this true old friend had ever done, still the relief to the elder sister—timid and mistrustful of herself as she was in the task before her—was none the less, and she plucked up sudden courage therefrom, and dashed boldly into the matter.

" Elsie, dear, I think I know why he was glad to get away—glad of the excuse of work at the surgery which Felix would willingly have done had he not guessed that his friend really wished to leave us. James Oliver has long been attached to you, Elsie, and you showed too much consciousness, on the sudden appearance of Edgar Carlyon, for him to doubt that at least a favorable impression had been made on your heart by that gentleman. I watched the whole scene," she went on hurriedly, and more nervously, as the little sister (never spoken to as a woman

till now) began to evince symptoms of astonishment and agitation ; "and I had been watching
him—James Oliver—for some time previous,
while you were singing to him ; and I am quite
positive that I am correct in what I tell you. Oh!
Elsie, darling, we still hope (Felix and I) that
you will choose the old rather than the new friend,
and not doom to disappointment and unhappiness one of the best, and kindest, and truest
hearts in the world."

Here the speaker paused and slid her arm
round the waist of her hitherto speechless
listener, who had knelt down beside her sister,
and was now trembling all over, while the bright
red had deserted her cheeks, and left them almost
·as pale as Joanna's own.

"I cannot believe this—I think you must be
dreaming, Jo. I never heard so strange a thing
—it cannot, cannot, be true—"

So Elsie was saying, in broken sentences, and
with her very lips white from the utterly new
emotions that were making war in her mind,

while Joanna stroked the wavy, unbound hair, and smiled—in her sad, melancholy fashion—softly and pityingly into the pretty upturned face.

"But it is true, my darling," she resumed presently, as Elsie seemed waiting for further confirmation of the "strange thing." "Felix has known it a very long time, and encouraged his friend to hope you would return his attachment. He bade me speak to you to-night ; he is so fond, you know, of James Oliver, so sure that he would make you happy. I believe this too, Elsie, if you could care for him enough to marry him. Oh, my darling, don't be misled by mere outward attractions, don't lightly cast from you a pure and faithful affection for the sake of a better position in society, or because it seems to you that flattery and external homage are signs of real love."

Bravely, kindly, faithfully, spoken! And yet destined to share the fate of almost all counsel that has ever been given under the sun, when it is opposed to the will or inclinations of the individual to whom it is addressed.

Elsie's tears were flowing fast (she was but a child and rather a spoilt one, after all) as she replied in unsteady accents to her sister's earnest appeal.

"Oh, Joanna, I wished I had known or guessed anything of this before to-day. Indeed, indeed, I always thought it was you that James Oliver liked. He is so grave, so good, so wise, and he and you agree on so many subjects. I am sure he esteems you and Felix above anybody in the world. Yet I believe I could have grown to love him had I suspected that he really cared for me, and was caring for me even while I was sick and dull, and a burden to all around me. Why did he not tell me himself; why am I only now to learn it, when—"

She stopped abruptly, and hid her burning face on Joanna's shoulder—Joanna, who was white and calm as a snow image, as she took up her little sister's broken sentence in tones of mild and sorrowful reproach.

"When you have given away your heart to the acquaintance of an hour—is it really so, Elsie?"

"Dear Jo," sobbed this foolish Elsie, "I never, never saw anybody like him; anybody who fascinated and charmed me in the same way. Don't tell a living creature that I have said this—don't mention it to me again. I am ashamed to have confessed it even to you; but it is the truth, and if I tried ever so now to like James Oliver, I know—I know, dear Jo, I should be always thinking of Edgar Carlyon. You would not have me consent to marry a man I could not love."

"No, no," said the elder sister, hastily. "I could not wish that, Elsie; but it is none the less unfortunate that you should have met this Mr. Carlyon. Felix does not admire him. To me he appears light, and wanting in manliness. No doubt he is handsome and even pleasing in manner.

But, oh, Elsie, dearest, think of comparing him
for one moment with James Oliver. I could not
do our friend such grievous wrong."

This was, perhaps, unwise on Joanna's part.
It gave Elsie an excuse for standing up as
champion of the young man thus depreciated;
and Elsie had one of those generous, unreflecting,
natures which gratifies itself in espousing the
cause of whatever is trampled on or unvalued.

She deemed her sister prejudiced and harsh
in her opinion of Edgar Carlyon, and took some
pains to prove that he was neither light nor
wanting in manliness. Had she not talked with
him the whole evening, and had he not given
abundant evidence of being intellectual, noble-
minded, tender-hearted, and, in short, all that a
frail mortal could be—without wings, and in a
superfine black coat?

Not that Elsie thus jested concerning his many
charming attributes, only she vindicated him so
warmly and enthusiastically in answer to her
sister's slighting comments, that Joanna, very

tired in body as well as mind, was led in the end to say—

"If he is but half the perfection you have painted him, Elsie, I can understand indeed that Mr. Oliver will stand a poor chance beside your new friend. But now, my child, let us go to bed. I have utterly failed, as I knew I should, in the task that Felix entrusted to me, and this failure distresses me too much to leave me any inclination for speaking more of it to-night. I am tired, Elsie."

Truly she looked so; and the younger sister, feeling very like a culprit, and yet conscious of a novel and secret gladness that triumphed over all, had no wish to continue the discussion. She undressed herself quickly, and was just creeping silently into bed, when it occurred to her to return and throw her arms round Joanna's neck, the latter still sitting in the same place where Elsie had found her, and with her books open, but as yet unread, before her.

"Darling Jo. I am more sorry than I can

tell you for all this, and especially for the pain I see it is giving you. If Felix asks about it to-morrow, you must not breathe a word on the subject of Edgar Carlyon—only assure him that I could not love Mr. Oliver well enough to marry him, while really liking him dearly as a friend, and being above measure grateful for all his past kindness to me; you will do this?"

"Elsie, I will not betray your confidence, but Felix will know, without a syllable from me, how it really is. We have, in truth, all been blind—all spoken too late. It is no fault of yours, dear—no fault of anybody's. According to our imperfect judgment of all human affairs it is a misfortune, the consequences of which I can only pray earnestly may not fall too heavily on my Elsie's head."

The little sister tried to smile through the tears that had re-commenced, but her companion's extreme gravity depressed her in spite of herself, and so she went to bed, and left Joanua to her reading and her prayers.

CHAPTER V.

THE WOOER AND THE WOOED.

Mr. Edgar Carlyon became almost a daily visitor at the house of his father's old partner. He had very few friends that he cared about in London, and living at an English hotel was rather slow for a young man accustomed to all the excitements of a continental life. The Pagets, though by no means a cheerful family taken *en masse*, were always friendly and agreeable to strangers, and one got excellent music and very tolerable dinners there, and that widow was really amusing with her solemn coquetries and her everlasting streamers: and poor Lillie, when by stratagem or determination she could escape from the tyranny of her own home, was piquante and interesting, and as for little Elsie, pretty little Elsie, there was no denying that she was excuse enough for any man, who had nothing else to do, turning his steps daily in the direction of the villa at Bayswater.

"Ah," sometimes replied Mr. Carlyon the elder, when his son would thus lightly yet candidly allude to his increasing intimacy with the Pagets, "they are all well enough, as you observe, when nothing more exciting is in the way, and I am glad you don't object to killing an idle hour or two with them now and then. That little girl with the bright coloured hair is certainly growing pretty as you remarked. She could be made something of in Paris, I dare say. When you have got a wife, Edgar, it will be a charity to ask her over to stop with you."

And then Mr. Edgar would flush up very hotly, and either speak immediately of something else or take out a cigar and puff away at it in silence.

Most satisfactory symptoms, as the anxious and plotting father complacently decided in his own mind, while discharging, weekly, very heavy bills at their hotel, and playing daily by himself the amusing game of patience.

In the meanwhile Dr. Paget and Joanna mourned over the loss of *their* game, and sympathized, heart and soul, with the friend they valued nearly equally. For in the family circle Mr. Carlyon's attentions to Elsie were now spoken of openly and constantly. The father and mother, and even Mrs. Vining when she was in a good humour, made no secret of their rejoicing in the prospect of such a connection, such a splendid match for darling Elsie, who would grace the highest station in the world and look so charming, the widow said, in black velvet and diamonds.

Felix and Joanna were both ordinarily silent when these conversations were being held. Once, in the very commencement, Felix had spoken out abruptly and sternly. He had said, addressing no one in particular—

" I should have thought there had been enough unhappy marriages in this family already, to have secured Elsie from being thrown into the arms of the first handsome adventurer who condescends to think her pretty, but I suppose we are a doomed race, or that poor child, at least, would have been spared."

Now as Dr. Paget, in his righteous indignation, went far beyond the truth in calling Edgar Carlyon an adventurer, his remonstrance did no good in any way.

Mrs. Paget had replied sharply—

" Where so many have made fools of themselves, it is the more desirable that one should do a wise thing."

And then her son, with no further retort, had turned on his heel and refrained thenceforth from any open interference.

With Elsie herself he had daily increasing experience of the uselessness of arguing. She loved Felix dearly, and had hitherto willingly accorded him an elder brother's privilege of advising and lecturing her in all matters that his years and gravity—gravity which so often passes for wisdom—seemed to qualify him for understanding and directing. To please him she had set about repairing the deficiencies of her education as soon as she was well out of the sick room ; she had practised dry and uninteresting music daily, she had read equally dry and uninteresting books; she had taken lessons in French and German, and finally, she had, under Joanna's superintendence, learnt the mysterious art of using a needle and thimble, and could mend her own gloves and stockings without any more serious consequences than pricking the little taper fingers till they were a sight to look at, and even her task master himself had compunctions about trying to convert so tender and pretty a thing as Elsie, into a common place, industrious woman.

But the day that brought Edgar Carlyon to Bayswater was the last of the brother's influence and authority. With the new and absorbing love that had sprung up in Elsie's heart, her whole nature seemed to change. The lightness and joyousness that had made her such a sunbeam in the house, had given place to a very quiet, gentle, preoccupied manner that, while less attractive to the gloomy spirits around her, was intensely suggestive of some deeper, stormier emotions than she had hitherto known, mingling in the current of her own life.

And not unwelcome! Oh, none could deem them otherwise than warmly, passionately received and cherished who took the trouble to read the soul's writing on Elsie's innocent face, day after day. Great happiness is never noisy, rarely demonstrative. It loves to sit shrouded in its own star-lined mantle, excluding the outer world, and more than content to gaze with joy flooded eyes at the world of beauty and of light that has opened upon it within.

So it was with Elsie, and Felix, seeing this, let her alone, and waited, not patiently but of necessity, to see how things would shape their course, and to be in readiness, should an opportunity occur even at the eleventh hour, to give his aid in expelling the intruder from their hearth and home, and bringing in his own friend in Edgar Carlyon's place.

For the present, James Oliver kept wholly aloof from the family. He was not a man to talk of his own disappointment, or to complain of having been badly used, even had it been clear that little Elsie had used him badly. What he suffered, he suffered in absolute silence, and even Felix could only dimly guess how dark the sun and the moon had grown to him since the night when he had listened dreamingly to Elsie's "fairy bells."

But Dr. Paget, with many virtues and excellencies, had a certain imperiousness of nature which made it very difficult for him to abandon anything on which he had strongly set his heart. He would not believe that this hateful marriage was even yet so sure a thing as the rest of the household appeared to think it. Edgar Carlyon doubtless admired Elsie exceedingly, and felt a warm interest in her society, but he had at present said nothing that could be construed into an assertion that he wished to marry her, and might he not, after all, turn out to be one of those brave and gallant heroes who love and who ride away?

The summer days were passing quickly. The roses had come and gone, and still no more could be recorded of Mr. Carlyon's elegant son than that he was a constant guest at the merchant's house, and, when there, little Elsie's shadow.

But Elsie herself had no misgivings. She knew from the very first, with woman's keen instinct in these things, what it all meant. And she was right; for ere a leaf had fallen from the acacia trees on the lawn, under which she and Edgar had so often sat, with only Hector to listen to their murmuring voices, there came a day when, the two Carlyons dining together, the younger abruptly said—

"Sir, you suggested once that as soon as I was married, it would be a charity to invite Elsie

Paget to come and stop with me awhile. Well, I have invited her to come and stop with me for life. I hope it meets your approval."

The sudden lifting of the elder gentleman's eyelids might possibly have had reference to the quaint manner of this announcement, but he was quite as well content that his son should attribute any surprise he-exhibited to the announcement itself. It formed no part of his tactics to show, even now, the nature of the game he had played and won. He only replied, therefore, after just such a natural pause for consideration as the circumstances seemed to demand—

"An odd choice, perhaps, for a man who has been about the world as you have, Edgar; but, upon the whole, you might have done worse. The girl will have twenty thousand pounds on coming of age."

"I know nothing about that," said Mr. Edgar, somewhat indignantly. "There can be no need, in my case, to look out for money with a wife.

I think the young lady will suit me, or I should not have chosen her."

"Of course, of course," added the father, lightly (Sly old fox! he was deeply and seriously content with what he heard), "and I am sure, Edgar, it will give me pleasure to welcome such a pretty little daughter-in-law. Here, my boy, fill your glass and let us drink her health—Sweet Elsie Paget, and long life and prosperity to her and her future husband!"

CHAPTER VI.

POOR LILLIE'S HOME.

THE same toast was given, in slightly different words, on the same day, in the Paget family. Mr. Paget proposed it, looking elated and even more complacent than was his wont; Mrs. Paget responded, filling her glass with her favourite port, and smoothing out the wrinkles on her brow in honour of the great occasion. Mrs. Vining took it up, helping herself and Master Arthur to some rather choice claret that stood near her, and Felix and Joanna, whatever their feelings, had no excuse for not uniting with the rest in wishing joy and prosperity to the dear little sister whose face of perfect and unclouded con-

tentment, shy and agitated as it was just now,
proved that she at least believed the destiny that
awaited her to be the brightest and the happiest
in the whole world.   Of course Elsie could
not but be aware of what was passing in the
minds of her brother and her favourite sister,
while they were gravely accepting the father's
challenge to drink her health—coupling her name
—as it must ever henceforth be coupled—with
that of Edgar Carlyon.   But strong in her own
faith in the man she had chosen, she believed the
time would speedily arrive in which they too
must acknowledge his worth—and after she had
thanked them all, with glad tears in her pretty
eyes, she turned and whispered to Felix, sitting
near her—

"I will not ask you to try and love what *I*
love, because I know you must do so in the end,
independently of me.   Oh Felix, he *is* good; he
is noble; he has qualities that those who know
him superficially would never guess at.   *I* know
him, and I respect as much as I love him."

Felix did not smile incredulously or contemptuously at this girlish speech. He did not smile at all; but he took the little hand that sought his under the table, and squeezed it tenderly without a word.

When somebody said presently what a pity it was that poor Lillie could not be of the family party to-day, Felix roused himself from a reverie into which he had fallen, and declared he had intended going to see her that evening, and he would, if possible, bring her back with him for an hour or two.

So as soon as Mr. Paget was left to his claret and his after dinner nap, and the ladies had settled themselves in the drawing-room to discuss the hundred and one interesting matters which a wedding in a family inevitably involves, Felix went out by the garden to his surgery, intending briefly to announce what had occurred to James Oliver, whom he was sure to find there, and then go on to pay a visit to Mrs. Wilmot.

Mr. Oliver was engaged in the unromantic

occupation of mixing some medicine for a poor woman who was seated in the surgery waiting for it, when his partner went in. He looked up on the opening of the door, nodded, and continued his work. When it was finished he labelled it carefully, gave it the patient, dismissed her, and then turned to his friend.

"You are here before your time, Paget"—he said in his ordinary voice—"Company at the house to-night?"

"No—nobody at all—but I am on my road to Mrs. Wilmot's. They want her at home. The women have something to talk about of more than common interest to them. Mr. Carlyon—"

"Yes, I know," interrupted James Oliver very quietly as far as the tone went, though Felix had seen the spasm that convulsed his lips for a moment—"I met your sister Joanna this afternoon at one of the almshouses, and on my enquiring how they all were at home she suddenly began to cry, poor girl! and then as I urged her to explain what ailed her, she told me what had occurred, adding that neither you nor herself liked Mr. Carlyon. I sincerely hope, Paget, you are both mistaken in your estimate of this gentleman, and that he will make your sister very happy. She deserves it."

These were Mr. Oliver's congratulations—all that he offered on the occasion. Felix shook him by the hand warmly and heartily, but not a word more was said by either of them on the subject. Dr. Paget only stayed to run his eye over a note or two that had been left for him from some of his most troublesome patients, and then, telling his partner that he should be back to release him in an hour, he started on his walk to his married sister's house, wondering, as he went, that Joanna should not have mentioned to him her interview with James Oliver.

Suddenly a new thought, a new suspicion, occurred to him, and in the sharp pain it occasioned, he stopped abruptly in his rapid walk, and remained for a minute or so looking gloomily and abstractedly at the swiftly passing vehicle on the road he was himself pursuing.

A Hansom cab dashed by, and close to him, while he thus stood lost in his own vexed musings. Two persons were in it—a woman and a man. The first had her back turned towards the pavement, that the energetic language she appeared to be holding might be the better heard by her companion, whose face was close to her own, and whose whole attitude expressed deep and absorbing interest in what she was saying. Felix had no idea whether the woman was young or old: they passed too rapidly for him even to be very sure that the garb was that of a lady. He only saw that the gentleman was Edgar Carlyon; and after one hasty, passionate exclamation, he continued his walk, bearing a heavier burden on his mind than ever.

The Wilmots lived in a small house in the neighbourhood of Paddington. When Lillie married, her husband had had an excellent position as partner in a wine merchant's business, and he had taken his young and pretty wife to a charming villa in the neighbourhood of St. John's Wood; but before the expiration of the first twelvemonth, Richard Wilmot, with the thoughtless folly which had ever characterised him, sold his interest in the concern, which was yielding him a certain though moderate income, and invested the whole sum thus realised in one of those bubble speculations that failed in its very infancy. His father-in-law, though justly incensed at what had happened, succeeded in finding him employment in another house of business, and for a year and a half things went on pretty steadily. Then the instability of Mr. Richard's character broke out afresh. Some elderly relation died, and left him five hundred pounds, just enough, he said, to enable him to commence a snug little business he had long had in his eye, on his own account. Accordingly, and against the urgent advice of Mr. Paget, and the entreaties of his wife, this snug little business was entered upon, and, in Mr. Richard Wilmot's hands, went, with his five hundred pounds, to the dogs in about nine months. Since then he had been fain to accept a subordinate situation in the establishment where he had once been partner—he had quarrelled hopelessly with all his wife's family; he had been compelled to take his wife into a smaller house in a less desirable neighbourhood; and, finally, he was fast learning to drown in wine or spirits the remembrance of his disappointments, and was only saved from becoming a confirmed drunkard by the fact that he was, and had ever been, a detestable glutton.

Such was poor Lillie Paget's husband, the man who, on her brother's entrance into the little dingy back parlour that evening, was found stretched at full length on a sofa, giving audible, though not particularly musical, tokens that his spirit (what there was of it) had departed for the time to other realms, and that there would be no fear of his overhearing anything that Dr. Paget might have to say to his sister.

Lillie was seated at a table near the open window—open probably less for the heat than that the fumes of tobacco and spirits with which the small room had been recently filled, might escape, and a purer atmosphere enter from without. She was using the fading daylight in looking over a parcel of tradesmen's books which were apparently perplexing her not a little. For as Felix was announced, and stood beside her, she swept them all with a great sigh of relief into the drawer of the table, and. giving her hand to her brother, said cordially :

"I am so glad to see you. I was getting fairly sick over my miserable accounts, which won't come right any how. How are they all at home? Of course, you have come to have a good long chat with me."

"I have come in the hope of taking you back to Bayswater," replied Felix, "glancing, with a movement almost of disgust, round the untidy room, though Lillie had cleared her own table, and there was even a vase of fresh flowers in the centre of it. "Do you think you can manage it?"

"Oh, I wish I dared," she said, in a low tone, that expressed less sorrow than indignation, and a tendency to rebellion; "but Dick has been fiercer than ever to-night, and until he laid down there and went to sleep, I scarcely felt my life was safe with him. I believe they have complained of his unpunctuality or something, at the office, and threatened to dismiss him. If they do this, Felix, and of course they will in the end, we *must* starve or go to the workhouse. Papa has sworn he will never help Dick again, and I should be glad to know who *would* help a man like that. For my part, I rather hope we *shall* starve; it might bring him to his senses; and nothing in the future can be much worse than the present is to me. With a child to love, I might bear it—I am no coward, as you know, Felix; but alone why should I? I don't mean to, a great deal longer, I can tell you."

"Lillie," replied Felix, looking, as he felt,

deeply pained, "I cannot bear to hear you talk in this way. I will not preach to you of its sinfulness as Joanna would do, though we both know quite well that it *is* sinful. But I know too, that there are trials and conditions in life against which the human heart will rebel, even should the rebellion be potent as the angel's two-edged sword to shut us out of paradise. I recognise your trial, my poor girl, as one of these ; and yet I say to you ' beware, Lillie,' or you will render it not only worse but irremediable. Do you think there is nothing you could do by your influence towards reforming your husband ?"

The wife uttered a short laugh, not bitter or contemptuous, for there was little of bitterness or contempt in poor Lillie's nature, but simply expressive of astonishment at what Felix had said—

"Joanna would tell me I have need to reform myself first," she replied; " and I believe she is right. Dick is a more open sinner no doubt, but I don't suppose his heart is much worse than mine, and I think sometimes, Felix, that less will be required of those in whose natures the animal triumphs so completely over the intellectual, as in the case there," glancing for a moment towards the sofa—" May we not, at least, hope as much ?"

" Perhaps," said Dr. Paget, a little absently, and as if he would gladly waive theological discussions just know; " but, Lillie, if you really cannot come with me, I must be bidding you good night as I have to relieve Oliver at the surgery before eight. I have not yet told you the great news you would have heard at home."

" Oh, no ; we have been wasting all this precious time in talking about my insiguificant troubles ; but it did not strike me that I was wanted at Bayswater for anything particular, or be sure I should have got at it sooner. I suppose I can guess, though. Little Elsie's admirer has spoken out at last, and they are going to launch that blessed child upon the stormy sea of matrimony. Poor darling ! if she should come to grief it will be an easier thing for me to break my heart for her than I have ever found it, or ever shall find it, to cry my eyes out on my own account."

"Well," rejoined Felix, laying his hand affectionately upon his sister's, as it rested for a moment on the table, "they are all in raptures at home about this great match that Elsie has secured. She herself is in love, and therefore fancies, poor little simpleton! that she is going straight into paradise. I don't like the man; nay more, I utterly mistrust him, and if by any influence of mine I could set it aside, even now, I would work night and day, and deem no trouble too severe, that might accomplish so important a purpose."

Dr. Paget spoke very warmly and emphatically, and his sister, discovering his strong opposition to the match in question, felt suddenly inclined, woman-like, to make the best of it.

"After all, Felix," she said, "he is a gentleman, a man of perfect refinement; and refinement in a husband will secure a wife against some of the worse evils in conection with matrimony." Here again she glanced—this time unconsciously—towards the sleeping brute on the sofa; "and I do think Mr. Carlyon is very sincerely attached to Elsie."

" No thanks to him for having taken a fancy to one of the sweetest and most artless children in the whole world," Felix exclaimed bitterly (there was plenty of bitterness in this character), " but what guarantee have we that his fancy will outlive the honeymoon ? I know it won't. I tell you I utterly mistrust the man, Lillie, and I could no more stand by and see her given to him at the altar than I could witness the striking off of her innocent head at the block. I shall go away when the marriage is to come off."

" And what does Joanna say to it all ?"

" Oh, Joanna does not like it much better than I do, but then she has less *reason* for her objection. She feels, I think, for poor Oliver, who loved that child, Elsie, as the apple of his eye ,

and would have sheltered and guarded her
through life as if she had been some precious gift
sent direct to him from heaven. Oh, the un-
utterable folly that is displayed in the choice of
husbands and wives. It makes one's very soul
sick to reflect upon it. Truly we do not need a
poet to tell us that—

'All things here are out of joint.'

But I must be gone now, Lillie, and you must
send home your promise to come as soon as you
possibly can, to Bayswater. Good night, dear."

"Oh, I am so sorry to lose you," sighed poor
Lillie, holding her brother's outstretched hands
tightly and yearningly, as if she dreaded the
solitude to which he would leave her. "But
just one word, Felix, before you go. Can't you
tell me what reasons you have for thinking ill of
this Edgar Carlyon?"

"No, Lillie, I cannot do that. I may tell
some of them to my father, but with small hope
of making any impression. There, I declare, is

eight o'clock striking, and I shall have to take a cab. Now shut the window, little sister, and have up candles. I do not like to leave you moping in this semi-darkness. Do you hear?"

"All right," replied brave Lillie, with a smile that somewhat reassured her brother (men judge so superficially of women) "and so, if you *must* go, good night, and take my love and a kiss to all at home. I will come the instant I can get away. Perhaps to-morrow, to their lunch."

"Mind you do," said Felix, and then he let himself out noiselessly, and hailing the first cab he saw, drove rapidly, but with his mind full of sad and foreboding thoughts, to the surgery.

CHAPTER VII.

A CAUTION MADE LIGHT OF.

FELIX PAGET had told his sister Lillie that he could not communicate to her the reasons he had for mistrusting Edgar Carlyon. He referred especially when he so spoke to the discovery he fancied he had made that evening—the discovery that Mr. Carlyon, while actually engaged to one lady, was carrying on a flirtation—to give it its very mildest name—with another. As a man of the world Dr. Paget was naturally inclined to regard very suspiciously the really suspicious incident which had accidentally come under his observation in reference to his future brother-in-law. As a man of strong prejudices he was not likely to take the most charitable view of any doubtful action on the part of an individual he had been pre-determined to think ill of. And thus it came about that in calmly, and, as he believed, dispassionately going over the matter in his own mind on his way home, Felix Paget arrived at the conclusion that the man to whom his gentle little sister was to be given in marriage—the man who was henceforth to hold her life's happiness in his hands, was not only frivolous, vain, and light of nature, but actually immoral—entangled in some disgraceful connection at the very moment when he was proposing to take a pure and almost child-wife to his heart and home.

Now Dr. Felix Paget, as may already have been seen, had a hundred faults and a vast number of weaknesses, but he had one quality which I think deserved the name of a virtue, and as such should have been counted as a set-off against many of his errors.

He had a very high and chivalrous notion of what was due to women of every rank and age and degree. He looked upon them as creatures to be guarded from the slightest breath or taint of impurity, and deemed that any man who spoke in the presence of his mother, wife, or sister, of the vices of his own sex, was guilty of something little less than sacrilege. Of course it followed naturally from this that he also held severe opinions concerning what a woman ought to be in thought, word, and action, and that the one who failed to reach his standard, whose mind could willingly admit the very faintest tinge of impurity, became thenceforth to him as a star that has lost its course, and as no more to be reckoned amongst the unsullied lights of heaven.

With regard to men, although a strictly moral man himself, he held that their laxity of principles was less a social than a religious evil, and while incapable of bestowing a grain of sympathy upon the feeblest law-breaker amongst them all, he still made a very broad distinction between their spot and the spot of those really weaker beings who, in his somewhat fanciful imagination, ought to prove themselves only a little lower than the angels.

Felix Paget certainly evidenced a superior order of mind in the high standard he had ever set up in respect to women; but he showed a flaw even in this nobility of nature, when he expected the weak and dependent to have more inherent power to stand upright than the self-reliant and the strong.

How all this worked will be seen more fully by and bye. It is mentioned here chiefly to explain his refusal to admit Mrs. Wilmot to his confidence on the subject of Edgar Carlyon's supposed vices, and why it was that he felt it would be almost easier and better to allow Elsie to risk her entire future with this man, than to sully her pure young ears now by such a tale as he might tell were he so disposed.

But there was no earthly reason why Elsie's father should not be informed of the circumstance which, in her brother's opinion, was so important and suggestive; there were indeed abundant reasons in favour of the communication being made with the least possible delay. So as soon as Dr. Paget could leave his post at the surgery for the night, he went in through the garden to the house, and, luckily for his purpose, found the head of the family alone, still enjoying the quiet nap in which his wife and daughters had left him when they went upstairs to bed.

"Anything the matter?" exclaimed the sleeper, waking with a start and speaking testily, as is the custom of elderly gentlemen disturbed in their pre-nocturnal slumbers—"what a row you make, my good fellow, in coming into a room. It's bed time isn't it?"

"I will detain you a few minutes, sir, if you please," replied Felix, taking a chair and drawing it beside that of his father. "I have a word to say to you that I could only say when we are alone. Has Carlyon been here to-night?"

Still smarting under the injury inflicted on him

in this abrupt intrusion on his nap, and running his fingers through his stiff and crumpled gray hair, Mr. Paget said shortly that he had of course been there. Had Dr. Paget anything to advance against so very natural a proceeding?

"I think it right to mention to you," resumed Felix, paying no heed to his parent's irritation, "that while I was on my way to the Wilmots this evening a Hansom cab passed me containing Mr. Edgar Carlyon and a female with whom he was evidently conversing in a most animated and energetic manner. I did not see the woman's face, but her figure was youthful, and I must add that the whole transaction wears, to my thinking, a most suspicious aspect."

"Anything more, my good fellow?" asked Mr. Paget, gradually recovering his equanimity, but speaking with a coolness most provoking to his excited listener—"anything more?"

"Is not that about enough, sir?" Dr. Paget asked, sternly; "enough to convince you that the gentleman to whom you were about marrying your daughter is altogether unworthy of her, is a heartless libertine, insulting a pure woman by his honourable proposals while he is engaged in a *liaison* with probably an opera dancer or something of that disreputable kind ?"

· It had not escaped Mr. Paget's observation (for he was very wide awake now) that Felix had spoken of Elsie's matrimonial prospects in the past tense, as if he had no doubt whatever that the communication he had now made would suffice tó set the matter altogether aside. If the son really did for one instant cherish such an idea, the father's first words in reply to what he had last advanced must at once have undeceived him.

"If you were not such a melancholy, unsocial fellow," he said, quite blandly and cheerfully, "I should really suspect you of having spent a convivial evening. This seems the most rational way of accounting for the nonsense which, upon my word, it appears to me you are talking."

Had Dr. Felix Paget yielded here to the passionate impulse of the moment, he would have turned on his heel and never said another word in his own family about the matter under dispute; but he was accustomed to command himself, and he had his little sister's future peace very strongly at heart; so he only hesitated a few seconds just to gulp down the indignation which his parent's words were undoubtedly calculated to excite, and then replied, in a voice as calm and cool as the other's—

"By whatever name you choose to designate the truths I have felt it right to bring before your notice, the fact remains that they *are* truths which every father who cared for his child's honour and happiness would think it, at least, worth while enquiring into."

"This is my concern, sir," retorted the father, beginning to show now that he was incensed at his son's interference; "and allow me to add that I am in no need of being reminded of my duty by you, or by any man breathing. It seems to me that if your mother and myself are satisfied with the character of the gentleman who has just been accepted by your sister, any frivolous objections on your part may easily be waived. Heaven knows it is not often that Mrs. Paget is satisfied about anything. When she is, I think the rest of the family may agree in the expediency of not altering the state of things which has happened to content her. And, after all, your fine story which appears to you so suggestive, suggests little to my mind but the old play of ' much ado about nothing.' "

Still keeping his temper admirably, because of what he believed to be at stake, Dr. Paget again said—

" It may be so, sir. I very sincerely hope it is ; but while there is the shadow of a chance that I am right in my conjectures I would entreat you not to dismiss the subject contemptuously from your thoughts, but rather to entertain it without prejudice, and, should the result of this be as I anticipate—a conviction that what I witnessed to-night was, at least, odd and suspicious—make enquiries before it is too late that shall set the question at rest for ever. You may even, if you please, mention to Mr. Carlyon what I have now told you, and require him to explain it. Elsie's happiness is of far more importance than the establishment of a friendly feeling between her future husband and myself."

Whether Mr. Paget was growing sleepy again, or whether his son's mildness and perseverance really had an effect upon him, it might be difficult to say ; but certain it was that after a prolonged yawn, which had succeeded Dr. Paget's last words, he said, with recovered blandness—

" Well, well, my good fellow, I give you credit for the best intentions, and I promise you, if that will make you happy, to have a talk with young Carlyon before he sees Elsie again. It would never do, as you say, to have that poor little girl made miserable, and, though my own mind is clear as to her lover's worthiness and the insignificance of what you saw this evening, still it won't do, for appearance sake, to have her future husband seen driving about with other women in

Hansom cabs. I am glad you mentioned his little imprudence to me, Felix; don't prate of it to the ladies. And now good-night, for I'm more than half asleep, and your mother has rung her bell these ten minutes."

Only half satisfied with what he had achieved, and yet feeling that it was better than nothing, Dr. Felix Paget went to bed also, and had uneasy dreams throughout the night concerning Elsie and Lillie, both of whom appeared to his excited imagination to be pursued by some hideous demon, which, every now and then, took the familiar form, not of Edgar Carlyon, but of Richard Wilmot.

CHAPTER VIII.

THE GUEST AT THE SURGERY.

MR. PAGET had not thought it necessary to mention to his son, during the conversation they had held together, the fact of his having overheard Edgar Carlyon tell Elsie he should be engaged, during the whole of the next morning, on business that could not be postponed, and that consequently she must not expect to see him till the evening.

But he perfectly remembered this circumstance all the time Felix was speaking, and he decided, before he went to sleep again that night, that he would go and breakfast with the Carlyons at their hotel in the morning, and ask Edgar to walk part of the way to the city with him afterwards.

The father who, as the reader already knows, was secretly delighted at the engagement that had just been contracted, received his old partner very graciously, and, assuming that he had come to talk with him about the business details of the marriage in contemplation, proposed that as soon as breakfast was over they two should proceed to the city together, leaving Edgar to follow his inclinations in an opposite direction.

"I think," Mr. Paget said, with his blandest and cheerfulest smile—"I must be rude enough to suggest an amendment to this kind proposal. You and I, Carlyon, are more used to discuss business matters over our desks than strolling along the streets under a bright September sunshine. Come to my office, if that suits you, about four to-morrow and dine with us afterwards. For this morning I will invite Mr. Edgar to be my companion as far as Temple bar."

"I am quite at your service till eleven o'clock,"

the younger gentleman replied, calmly and cour-
teously ; and the elder one, not sorry to be spared
the necessity of leaving his cigar and his newspaper so early, smiled perfect approval of this new
arrangement,as he rang for breakfast to be brought
up immediately.

It happened that afternoon that Dr. Felix Paget
was summoned to attend a patient who had met
with a severe accident five or six miles out of
London.   He did not get back even to the surgery
until it was too late to join the family dinner
party, so he sent to the house for a dish of any
cold meat they happened to have, and, taking a
bottle of wine from the cupboard, invited James
Oliver, who had been kept from *his* dinner by his
partner's long absence, to share with him this
homely and unceremonious meal.

" With much pleasure and satisfaction," Mr.
Oliver replied, as a servant appeared carrying a
tray not unsubstantially laden. " I have been
too busy to remember that I was hungry till now,
but the name of dinner brings the fact to my

mind. We have had quite a little drama enacting at the surgery to-day, Paget."

Felix finished the loading of his friend's plate, pushed the wine to him, and then, before he helped himself to anything, asked somewhat anxiously for an explanation.

"This is it," resumed Mr. Oliver, who was not, apparently, even yet too hungry to be able to discuss professional matters. "I was busy looking over our books about four o'clock, when there came a faint uncertain ringing of the surgery bell. I thought it must be a small child, sent on some errand for a lazy mother, and I rose in a great hurry, not to keep the little thing waiting outside. I pulled open the door quickly, and in doing so, received, almost into my arms, the form of a lady, young, very handsome, rather shabbily dressed, and evidently suffering from a sudden attack of faintness, which I at once concluded had led her to our door. Well, I placed her first of all in a chair, took the liberty of untying her bonnet and removing her veil, and

then asked her what was the matter. The difficulty she had in answering me, and in begging
for a glass of water, convinced me that she was
strongly hysterical, and finding that after the
water, to which I added a pretty powerful dose of
ammonia, that she grew no better, it occurred to
me that I could not do a wiser thing than send
for your sister Joanna, who appears to understand and sympathise with every form of human
suffering. So I told the boy, who had luckily
come in just before, to run to the house and tell
Miss Joanna what had happened, entreating her,
if she was disengaged, to step round for a moment,
and see what she could do. You know, Paget,"
the narrator added apologetically, " I am in no
sense of the word a lady's man, and I really felt
something more than awkward and helpless in
the novel circumstances in which I was placed. In
a few minutes after the departure of my messen-
ger, I was startled by the abrupt entrance of your
youngest sister, looking half frightened, poor
child, but explaining that they were all out ex-

cept herself, and that she thought she might be better than no one. My patient, who till now had been lying back exhausted, and at times gasping as if for breath, on the easy chair, now opened her eyes, and as Elsie timidly offered her services, gazed at her with an interest and admiration that were apparent even through the weakness and mental agitation of some kind which would have made most women indifferent to everything around them. To tell you the truth, Paget, I was so taken up for the moment in admiring them both,—one does not often see two such lovely women together—that I did not hear what first passed between them. I only gathered that your sister had been proposing the removal of my fair patient to the house, by observing the startled look, and catching the peculiarly decided tones of the latter as she said—

"'No, no, no; not for the world; but I thank you all the same, for wishing it. You are very kind and good. I shall ever remember you with gratitude.''

"Then she took Elsie's hand and held it long, without speaking, in her own, and all the time great tears were coming down her pale checks like rain, and your sister, while evidently deeply interested, seemed as puzzled as I was to know what to do for the poor lady, and I expected and dreaded every minute to see her begin crying too, for sympathy. At last it suggested itself to me to ask if I might send to let the lady's friends know where she was, or if she would prefer my calling a cab, and seeing her safely home. 'I have no friends,' she replied then, in a voice of pathetic sadness that was very striking, 'but I am better now, and can get home to my lodgings unattended. I will not have a cab; walking is good for me. I shall not be faint again, or if I am (and here she turned to your sister, with that look of earnest interest deepening in her face) 'the remembrance of your gentle kindness and compassion will revive me. Tell me your name, that I may mingle it henceforth in the least sad and bitter of my thoughts—

one day, perhaps, when I may dare to pray, in my prayers.'

"I thought this odd, you see," continued Mr. Oliver, "because, really, she did not give one the very faintest idea of being otherwise than a pure and virtuous woman ; but her last words shocked and distressed me on your sister's account, and my strongest wish now, was to get rid quietly of our mysterious visitor. Elsie told her name, as of course she could not help doing, and before I could have had a chance of preventing it, even had my interference been admissible, the stranger had thrown her arms round your sister's neck, and was kissing her even passionately. I really don't know, Paget, what you or any other man would have done under the circumstances,—much better, I have no doubt, than I did—*My* only thought at the instant was that a girl, pure and spotless as the angels in Heaven—a girl just emerged from childhood, and whose imagination could never have been sullied by one breath or suspicion of evil, was being held in the arms and pressed to the heart of a woman who, however beautiful to the outward eye, *might be*—I only went as far as that, Paget—might be defiled and stained within. I can't tell you what this thought, momentarily as it flashed across my mind, was to me. It made me shiver all over, and, acting on the quick impulse it excited, I seized Elsie's hand the instant that strange being had released her, drew her outside the surgery door, and entreated her to return home immediately, adding (for I knew not what other explanation of my conduct to give) that I feared the sick lady was not quite right in her head, and that I myself would now see to her being safely disposed of. Your sister obeyed me instantly without a question, though her wondering eyes and flushed cheeks testified to the excitement all this had occasioned her; and then I returned, for I ought to have told you that I saw Elsie across the road and safe into her own garden—I returned to the surgery, to make the best apology I could to the lady I had left, and, to my astonishment and

dismay, found that the bird had flown. Paget, I
give you my word that I never felt so guilty or
conscience-stricken in my life, as when I stood
gazing round that untenanted room, and picked
up a glove—here it is—that the poor thing had
dropped in her eagerness, I suppose, to get away.
She must have understood what was in my mind
when I almost dragged Elsie from her, and, if
my suspicion was without foundation, *think* what
she must have suffered under it. I was so heartily
ashamed of myself now, so bitterly sorry for
having driven her out alone in her weakness and
helplessness, that I seized my hat, and, heedless
of everything else, ran nearly half a mile up the
road towards London—of course in vain, as she
had probably taken the first vehicle she saw, and
been driven east, west, north, south—how should
I know—how shall I ever know now? And this
is all, Paget, and I am waiting for you to tell me
that I have behaved like the veriest ass that ever
ate thistles for his daintiest food. You are looking grave enough to have formed an even worse

opinion of me than this. Speak out, old fellow, and don't spare calling names, if that will relieve you."

But Felix Paget appeared in no mood either for calling names or for speaking out. He had listened with the deepest and most wrapt attention to every word of his friend's recital, and now that it was finished he sat supporting his head on one arm, and gazing, apparently with complete abstraction, at the little dark kid glove which James Oliver had passed over to him when he came to that part of his story. His countenance was, as his friend had said, very grave indeed; but it was something more than this—it was perplexed, it was bitterly indignant, it was sternly sorrowful, all at the same time. At length he lifted his eyes, fixed till now either absently or with very curious observance, upon the glove beside his yet untouched plate, and turning them to Mr. Oliver, said quietly—

"You did exactly what I should have done, James, only I think I should have been quicker in doing it. These beautiful daughters of Eve who wander about London alone are certainly not the kind of women whose friendship either you or I should covet for our wives or sisters. It was a pity that child Elsie came. I am not sure that I quite approve of your having sent for Joanna, but you did it for the best; you could not know—"

Here the doctor paused abruptly, and seeming to forget his audience, took up his knife and fork and began to eat rapidly, but not at all as if he was in any way enjoying, or likely to derive any benefit from, his food.

"And I do not even now *know* anything against this lady," spoke up Mr. Oliver presently, and appearing a little, just a very little annoyed at his partner's strange manner; "besides, I fancied I had made you distinctly understand that no shadow of a doubt as to her perfect respectability had even glanced across my mind until your sister had been quite five minutes in the room with her. Believe me I esteem Miss Joanna

Paget far too highly to have exposed her willingly to questionable society, though I am aware her creed teaches her that it would be sin to shrink from a fallen sister when there was the remotest chance of doing her any physical or moral good. I have heard her say as much many times, and yet I should be as reluctant as yourself to see her labours of love and duty exercised in this direction. You must not think, Paget, that it is only Elsie I would have spared."

"I think nothing, Oliver," replied the other, "that ought for a moment to offend or distress you; but I am worried, displeased, put out, about half a hundred things just now, and my mind is not quite so clear, nor my temper quite so serene as would be essential for pleasant companionship. Take some wine, however, and then pass the bottle. I want to go round and speak to the governor by and bye. I shall not be absent more than a quarter of an hour, and after that I can take your place here for the whole evening."

As James Oliver perceived clearly that he was

not to be taken into his friend's confidence concerning any of the half hundred things that were worrying and displeasing him, he prudently forbore to ask questions, but during the short time that they remained together talked on general subjects, avoiding instinctively (for he could see no *reason* why it should be avoided), any further allusion, direct or indirect, to the subject of his mysterious guest of the afternoon.

CHAPTER IX.

THE INTERVIEW IN THE LIBRARY.

EVERYBODY knows how common a thing it is for a person who has adopted a certain theory in explanation of any facts that have come before his notice to make every new incident that seems in the slightest degree capable of connection with these facts, bear out and support his own ideas in reference to them. To Felix Paget it appeared as clear as noonday that the lady of the hansom cab and James Oliver's guest were one and the same individual. Hence his reluctance to discuss the matter openly with his friend (whom at present he did not deem it advisable to admit to his confidence), and hence too his apparent lack of curiosity in not asking for a more minute description of the stranger whose beauty Mr. Oliver had so warmly eulogized. What motive this person could have had in presenting herself at the surgery he was at quite a loss to imagine—accident he could not believe it to be, in spite of his partner's testimony as to the reality of her illness. The extraordinary interest she manifested in Elsie seemed easier of comprehension, and while he shuddered at the thought of the familiar embrace to which his pure little sister had been exposed, he could not choose—as a humane and deeply sensitive man—but pity the unhappy woman who, whatever her sorrows or her wrongs, showed no bitterness or resentment towards one whom she probably too well knew had supplanted her in the affections of the inconstant being she doubtless loved and clung to, still.

It was nearly nine o'clock that night when Felix Paget walked into the hall of his father's house, his sole object being to see Mr. Paget and learn whether he had kept his promise in reference to Edgar Carlyon.

Apparently he had, for that young gentleman had dined with the family, and was now sitting in the small inner drawing room with Elsie, showing and explaining to her a book of fine engravings—scenes in France and Italy—which he had brought and presented to her, as his first lover's offering, that evening.

Felix learned as much as this from his sister Joanna, to whom he stopped to speak a few words on entering the room where most of the family were assembled; and then he went to his mother's sofa to enquire whether his father was at home and at liberty to grant him a short interview.

"I believe you will find him in the library, and alone," said Mrs. Paget, speaking querulously, and not even looking up from a newspaper on her lap—"but I shouldn't advise your worrying him with any business matters to-night, for something has put him out in the city, and he's as cross and disagreeable as he can well be."

"Everybody in the house is as cross and disagreeable as they can well be;" added Mrs· Vining with a face and in a voice that made it impossible not to include her in the category—"and if Mr. Carlyon were not too much in love to notice anything beyond Elsie, he would certainly have found out to-day that we are a most gloomy and unpleasant family. I wish, Felix, while you are at home this evening you would feel Arthur's pulse—the poor child is so fretful that I am sure something is the matter with him. I am horribly afraid of scarlet fever, and shouldn't wonder if he's sickening for it."

"Rubbish!" exclaimed Mrs. Paget with less courtesy and elegance than should have belonged to so fine a lady—"it's temper that is the matter with your boy, Georgina ; and if Felix has any prescription for *that* ailment, he'd better write out half a dozen, and distribute them to the household."

.As these sort of altercations, especially between Mrs. Paget and her widowed daughter, were things of daily, almost hourly, occurrence in the family, Dr. Paget took no sort of notice of the present squabbling. He only said, addressing Mrs. Vining—" I will look at Arthur if you wish it ;" and then, as if the subject had already passed from his mind, he enquired whether Lillie had been to Bayswater during the day.

" She came to lunch, poor thing !" returned the mother in a somewhat gentler voice—" and we all thought her in bad spirits. She did not acknowledge that she was, though, and before she left us, after we had gossiped for above an hour over Elsie's brilliant prospects, she was quite herself again. Lillie is a brave, good girl, one in a thousand. Nine hundred and ninety-nine women in her place would run away and leave that brute to manage as he could without her. Lillie has an admirable temper ; anyone might live peaceably with *her* to all eternity."

It scarcely needed the emphasis on the personal

pronoun to show that this last observation was spoken at Mrs. Vining, who, quick to understand the implied reproach, retorted with kindling cheeks.

"Poor Lillie is tried enough, Heaven knows! but she has never yet been tried by finding herself looked upon as an interloper, a something which it would be very pleasant to get rid of, in her own family. She has never eaten the bitter bread of dependence both in her own person and in that of her innocent child ; she has never been scowled upon for every bit of new ribbon or pair of clean gloves she may venture to put on, because the money for them does not come out of her own pocket ; she has never—"

"I had better go and find my father," interrupted Felix, not careful to conceal how heartily sick he was of these oft repeated scenes, "I will speak to the evidently happy pair in the next room when I come back. They are as yet quite unconscious of my presence."

In passing Joanna's chair Felix looked down at

her, as she worked, and was struck by the exceeding weariness and sadness of her aspect; it was always quiet and grave, but to-night it seemed to express an utter hopelessness and listlessness, as if—so at least her brother thought—some new and hidden anxiety were crushing out the little spirit there was ever in her.

"What's the matter, Jo?" he said, stopping for a minute and bending kindly over her, "you are suffering in some way, I am certain."

"I am very well," she replied, glancing up at her brother with a grateful smile that for the instant quite illumined her face, "and (in a lower voice), "I don't suppose that I suffer much more than you do in witnessing the constant strife that goes on around us—except," and here the dull, brooding look settled on her countenance again—"except, Felix, that I am ever mourning my own utter inability to do the least good in this unhappy household."

"My dear girl," her brother said a little impatiently, "this is making unto yourself an unnecessary affliction indeed. Why should you expect to do any good? I don't, and I am nearly ten years older than yourself, and ought to be ten years wiser. Of course you might talk and preach till voice and strength failed you, and nobody would pay the least heed to a word you said : but this need not make you unhappy, you foolish girl; it is no fault of yours."

No fault of hers! Joanna was not going to argue the point with Felix, for she knew she should only be as one speaking to him in an un-known tongue. She only sighed therefore and resumed her stitching, while her brother, deeming perhaps that his·common sense had put to flight some of his sister's odd crotchets, passed on to his eagerly desired interview with Mr. Paget in the library.

Very intent was that gentleman over his books and papers as his son, in answer to the somewhat churlishly given permission to enter, walked in and approached the library table.

"They told me I should find you here, sir," he

said abruptly, "and as I must be back at the surgery in less than half an hour I have ventured to intrude upon you for the purpose of asking the result of your interview—I presume you have had one—with Mr. Carlyon. For myself, I am even less inclined to think well of him at the present moment than I was last night. I wish from my heart—"

Something in the countenance of his listener must have suddenly arrested Dr. Paget, at this stage of his intended communications; for he not only came to a full stop, but his own face took an expression of wonder and almost of consternation as Mr. Paget looked up from his writing, and fixed his eyes on those of his son.

"Felix, I should have been glad," he began, in a rather laboured voice, "to have been spared this interruption to-night, and about a matter which is comparatively trivial—I at least think it so. Be at rest, however, on the subject of Edgar Carlyon's morality. I have talked with him, and received his solemn assurance that he is free from entanglements of any kind, that Elsie is the first woman he has ever loved. When he had told me this, with a quiet, earnest dignity that made it impossible for me to doubt his word, I felt that it would be simply insulting him to mention either your suspicions or their origin. Let me advise you to view the matter we discussed last evening in a more charitable light, and to cultivate friendly feelings towards the gentleman who will assuredly, in a few weeks, stand to you in the relation of brother."

"In a few weeks?"

Felix repeated these words almost mechanically, for, in truth, startling as it was to him to hear that Elsie's fate was so soon to be decided, there was that in his father's countenance and tone of voice which afforded more serious food for immediate thought than even the marriage which was so especially repugnant to him.

"Yes, in a few weeks I hope and have every reason to believe it will be," replied Mr. Paget significantly; adding, after a minute's pause, during which, though his eyes went down to his writing again, Felix could plainly see that some hot blood was suffusing his face, " nothing but this can save us all from utter ruin.   I am on the very eve of bankruptcy."

If Dr. Paget betrayed less astonishment and dismay at this announcement than an announcement of so serious a nature was naturally calculated to excite, it was probably because of the revelation made to him when he had first looked into his father's countenance that evening. Doctors as well as lawyers acquire in their profession a keen habit of observation, and it is not very difficult for them to guess, in scrutinising a human face, when the one cord has been struck which, above all others, can thrill with anguish or bitterness through every fibre of that particu- lar nature.

Felix possibly knew that it would be a lighter and an easier thing for the elderly gentleman, sitting with bowed head in that library chair to-night, to stand over the graves of all his nearest and dearest on earth, than it was for him to endure the contemplation of loss of position, and the frowns of a world that has ever chosen poverty to head its list of crimes.

In answer to the communication his father had now made to him, he said in a tone of great concern and sympathy :

" I deeply regret to hear that things are so bad as this with you, sir. I have thought for some time they were mending. I wish it were in my power to offer you any efficient help. I can certainly double what I have hitherto contributed as my share towards the maintenance of the establishment. My practice has been steadily increasing of late, and——"

It was almost with irritation that Mr. Paget here interrupted him. " Felix, you mean well, and I am much obliged to you for your liberal suggestion ; but, my good fellow, you know less than nothing of business, with its vast requirements and responsibilities. The whole of your income would be but as a drop in the ocean to meet my necessities just now. I have been systematically unlucky ever since Carlyon left the firm. If Elsie's money had been attainable at the present moment, and I could have used it as I liked, it is just possible that I might once more have weathered the storm; but you know as well as I do that in addition to the fact of her Godmother's legacy being securely tied up, she will not be entitled to it for another two years. I cannot wait another two months for help, and these Carlyons are my only hope and refuge."

He looked very wearied and harassed as he concluded this statement, and Felix felt, for the first time, that the cause he had so much at heart, and which he had entered that room once more to plead, was indeed a lost one.

He only asked now in what way his father counted upon Elsie's marriage for getting him out of his difficulties, and whether the Carlyons were at all acquainted with the state of his affairs.

"I believe," Mr. Paget replied, "my old part- ner guesses something near the truth. I mean to tell him all when he comes to-morrow. A word from him to the people I am connected with—to my principal creditors in short—will save me for the present; and for the future we must hope for the best. Elsie's marriage to so wealthy a man as Edgar Carlyon will assist me in many ways that I need not now enter upon. I am worn out for to-night, and those women in the other room worry me to death with their endless quarrels and complaints. If you could find a husband for Georgina Vining," he added, with a sudden effort to throw off business cares, and substitute domestic ones, "you would be doing me the greatest service, Felix, that one man ever rendered to another."

" By the bye," said Dr. Paget, feeling that no possible good could be gained by prolonging this interview, " Georgina thinks her boy is ill, and has asked me to go up and look at him. Perhaps I had better wish you good night, and attend to her request at once. Oliver will be expecting me back."

"Good night," said the father, holding out his hand and looking much relieved at the thought of being left alone again. "We will talk about that suggestion you made of doubling your present contribution when this ugly cloud has blown over."

CHAPTER X.

FAMILY SQUABBLES.

THERE was nothing very seriously wrong with Master Arthur Vining, nothing to justify his mother's anxious fears on his account, but she took occasion, while standing with her brother Felix beside her son's crib, to express in plainer terms than she had done down stairs her utter dissatisfaction with her position in her father's house, and to add, womanlike (under circumstances of real or fancied grievance), that she wished with all her heart she was dead and buried, for then she should be in nobody's way.

" Don't you think," said Felix, with whom it

was the rarest thing to interfere in the family disputes, "that if you tried to command your temper a little more, your life would be easier and pleasanter to you.   Depend on it, Georgina, we are all of us in a great measure the makers or the marrers of our own happiness.   There is no absolute reason why your position here should be so very painful an one as you represent it."

"All very fine talking," answered the lady, with kindling cheeks, " but let me tell you, Mr. Felix, you must be *in* the water before you can judge how cold it is.   As for my temper, which you so politely remark upon, it is sweetness itself compared with mamma's.   I should be glad to know who *could* command themselves living with her."

" Joanna manages it," said Felix, "and yet I think she gets quite as many hard and hasty words as yourself; and I believe, too, that her temper is not naturally a very good one."

" Joanna we all know to be a saint," retorted Mrs. Vining, bitterly, "and, therefore, she is bound to turn the left cheek when she is smitten on the right. For my part I make no professions of sanctity—nobody can accuse me of that—and I don't see why I should put up with the abuse I am continually getting. I really don't dare order Arthur a new dress or hat now. Even my father looked as black as thunder this afternoon when my last little bill at the milliner's was brought in, and mamma has been telling me that I spend more on dress during the year than she does."

"Georgina, are you aware," asked her brother gravely, "that our father's affairs are in a most unsatisfactory state; that it has become absolutely requisite for him to look closely even into the expenditure of his household? Perhaps this may be the reason of his receiving your milliner's account with disapproval to-day. Mr. Paget is not in general an illiberal man."

"How should I know anything about his affairs?" exclaimed Georgina, crossly; "nobody ever tells me anything; and, to speak frankly,

Felix, I don't believe a word about his being in difficulties. Men always swear they are, when they think the women in their family spend a threepenny-piece too much. Besides," she added, with charming consistency, "this is really no business of mine. When I had the great misfortune to lose my own home, and was asked to come back here, it was, of course, on the understanding that I was to be supplied with dress as well as with all other necessaries, and until I am dead and buried (which, as I said before, I should be glad to know would take place to-morrow), I shall claim my rights, in the teeth of all the black looks and hard speeches in the world."

Felix having nothing to reply to this spirited sentiment, not feeling justified without his father's permission in speaking more definitively· concerning those embarrassments in which *he* fully believed, told his sister that his time was up, and that he must return to the surgery. He would send or bring in a cooling draught for Arthur, and no doubt the child would be all right again in the morning. He had simply over-eaten himself, as spoiled, wayward children are apt to do, and was a little flushed and feverish in consequence.

Mrs. Vining accompanied her brother to the drawing-room, bidding Joanna, as she went in, light the piano candles for her, in the hope, perhaps, that music might charm away the savage spirit that had been tormenting her all the afternoon. In the meanwhile Felix walked to the inner room, said a civil word or two to Mr. Edgar Carlyon, a kind one to Elsie, and then, with a brief good night to all the party, retired to his duties at the surgery, and to a silent communing with those troubled thoughts which, after his friend had left him to himself, grew sadder and gloomier every moment.

The next morning, Dr. Paget was up early, and, in passing Elsie's room, he tapped at her door, and asked her if she would make haste down to the breakfast parlour, as he wanted to speak to her.

"You are so monopolized, little lady," he said to her on her speedy appearance, and after the morning greetings (affectionate ones always between Felix and Elsie) had been exchanged; "that one can never get a chance of speaking a word to you nowadays. I want to ask you about the occurrence at the surgery yesterday. James Oliver was telling me something of it last evening. What sort of a woman was she, Elsie?"

"A woman!" exclaimed Elsie, quite indignantly. "She was a lady, Felix, a perfect lady, and so pretty. I never saw so sweet looking a creature in all my life; surely Mr. Oliver would have said as much as this."

"He said she was handsome certainly, but I did not ask for details from him. I want you, Elsie, to give me some description of her. Was she fair or dark, short or tall, pale or ruddy? You women have keen eyes for minute points regarding each other's personal appearance."

"I have not, at any rate," Elsie answered, laughing. "If my life depended on it, I could never tell you whether my beautiful lady of yesterday had light or dark hair, blue or black eyes. I know that she was very, very pale, but then she had been nearly fainting, which would quite account for her want of colour. I am sure, too, that her eyes were soft and lovely, and her mouth small and full; beyond this, Felix, I noticed nothing, for the whole scene passed so rapidly, and astonished me so much that I was quite confused. I wish I could have persuaded her to come into the house with me."

"I don't," said Felix, abruptly; "but, Elsie," he continued presently, "she kissed you, I understand. Was not that an odd proceeding on the part of an utter stranger?"

"I—suppose—it was," replied Elsie hesitatingly, and as if she had scarcely so deemed it before. "Mr. Oliver must have considered it a liberty, I imagine, for he hurried me out of the surgery immediately afterwards, and I had not even a chance of saying good-bye to my new friend. Why was he so foolish, Felix? I am sure I regarded it quite as an honour to be kissed by such a very lovely and interesting woman."

"It is you who are foolish, Elsie," bluntly exclaimed her brother, "for not discerning the impropriety this person was guilty of. Mr. Oliver did well in sending you away. My little sister," he added, in a gentler tone, "must not take upon trust every pretty woman she may accidentally be brought in contact with. Unfortunately, this great city abounds in lovely women, whose kisses even upon your hand I should consider defilement, Elsie. I much fear the visitor of the surgery-was one of these."

A sudden tide of crimson rushed to Elsie's cheek as the first faint suspicion of her brother's meaning dawned upon her pure mind.

"Felix," she uttered, in a low, steadfast voice, "I am positive you are wrong. If ever innocence and goodness dwelt in any human heart they dwelt in the heart of that sweet lady who kissed me yesterday. I could stake my life upon it."

Dr. Paget smiled pityingly but very fondly into his little sister's face.

"We won't enter into an argument on this subject, dear," he said; "but later days may convince you that innocence and goodness often appear written on a woman's countenance long after those attributes have for ever deserted her soul. One other question, Elsie, and then I shall have done with you. Did you relate your little adventure to Mr. Carlyon?"

"No," said Elsie, while again the warm blood mantled in her cheek; "for I thought—I did not know—but I thought he might consider it odd my going to the surgery when you were not there; besides, it was scarcely a matter that would have interested him."

To this Felix made no answer at all, and soon after the other members of the family came down to breakfast, and subjects of a more general interest claimed his outward attention, if not his thoughts.

"You may as well ask Oliver to dine with us

to-day," observed Mr. Paget to his son while putting on his hat and gloves to start for the city—"there will be room at table, and he has scarcely been introduced to the Carlyons yet."

"I suppose we shan't succeed in getting poor Lillie this time," said the mother, frowning at her husband for the suggestion he had just made, evidently without consulting her, "otherwise there would *not* be room at table, Mr. Paget. You always *will* take things for granted."

"You know you told me yourself that Lillie would not be suffered to come," answered the master of the house rebukingly—"and even could she do so, room would easily be made by dispensing with Master Arthur's society for once. I wonder indeed, considering how prone that child is to eat unwholesome things, that you don't always arrange for him to get his meals early; it would be far better for him in every respect."

Having had his say, the head of the family hurriedly departed, quite unconscious that he left his eldest daughter in a fit of violent hysterics, which rendered nearly unintelligible the passionate language she was striving to pour forth expressive of the bitter wrongs and insults she was daily receiving, and the climax of which had been reached in Mr. Paget's cool suggestion that her darling Arthur should take his meals henceforth alone.

" I would marry a chimney sweeper if he would only ask me," this injured lady went on to declare—" and think my position an honorable and a happy one compared to that which I now occupy. I can't bear it much longer, and I won't. Many a woman has thrown herself into the Serpentine for troubles infinitely smaller than mine. *I* shall probably not need such a resource, for these daily and hourly worries are killing me as fast as ever they can. If Elsie does not make haste over her wedding, there may chance to be a funeral in the family first."

The renewed burst of tears that succeeded this allusion to her own possible decease, was scarcely reconcileable with Mrs. Vining's recent assertion that to be dead and buried was the summit of her ambition; but as nobody could accuse this lady of consistency any more than they could accuse her of professing to be a saint, her louder crying excited no astonishment, only Mrs. Paget, having grown tired of it, said sharply—

"You had better retire to your own room, Georgina, if you *must* make a fool of yourself. Mr. Paget is quite right about that boy. He gets to look heavier and more bloated every day, and it's from nothing in the world but late dinners and unwholesome food. You'll be losing him if you don't take care."

This was touching the one sole string in Georgina Vining's nature, which, so struck upon, could give forth a note of true and genuine pain. She really loved her child—not wisely, not even consistently, not with the sort of love which would be likely to benefit greatly the object on whom it was conferred—but still very dearly, very tenderly, and all the more absorbingly because he was the only thing in the wide world she could exclusively call her own. It is a mistake to suppose that because a woman is ill-tempered, discontented, occupied generally about trifles, and otherwise calculated to make those around her miserable—it is, I say, a mistake to suppose that such a woman is altogether incapable of strong affections. She may it is true pass through life without having her deepest feelings called forth, or, having been once called forth and disappointed, they may thenceforth slumber for ever; but it certainly often happens that the *capacity* for loving some one object strongly exists in the natures which appear to superficial observers wholly selfish and wholly trivial.

The sudden whiteness that Mrs. Paget's last observation brought to her widowed daughter's cheek—a whiteness observable even through the ugly blotches her tears had left, proved how swiftly the arrow had gone home and how sharp its point had been.

Mrs. Vining said not a word in answer—words were all very well for trifling grievances—but pushing back her chair with a vehemence that startled all at table she made a hasty retreat from the room, and sobbed out the rest of her passion by Arthur's bed, the child, in consequence of his indisposition of the previous night, having been indulged with his breakfast before rising.

"What a temper!" exclaimed Mrs. Paget, with uplifted eyes, as the door closed on Mrs. Vining; "I'm sure it's worth ten thousand a year to have such a daughter returned upon one's hands. If you could do anything towards correcting your elder sister's disposition, Joanna" (with a severe glance towards the second daughter) "it would be a better work and a clearer evidence, in my eyes at least, of your own piety, than railing at worldly amusements, and giving tracts to old apple women."

Mrs. Paget's tongue was certainly wonderfully successful this morning in uttering words that could cut right through the hearts of the individuals to whom these words were addressed. Joanna, indeed, had many vulnerable points, but none at the present moment more vulnerable than that which her mother had just reached—her very keen sensitiveness on the subject of her personal uselessness in her own family. She was not, however, given to retort or scold like Mrs. Vining, and although she did not literally turn the left cheek to be smitten with the right, she generally managed to receive hard words in silence, and to acknowledge to herself that if not agreeable they might in the end be wholesome.

Elsie, who was a little too much in awe of her mother (though *she* never got even a cross look from her) to interfere openly for either of her sisters, came round presently to where Joanna was sitting, and twined her arm caressingly round her sister's bowed neck.

"Dear Jo," she whispered, as their mother turned to give an order to a servant who had come into the room, "you can't work miracles, can you, any more than the rest of us?—but you are a good, patient darling, and when I have a home of my own you shall come and live with me, and we will be as happy as the day is long."

"Elsie," said Joanna (for now Mrs. Paget had gone out and the sisters were alone), "it is not happiness I covet for myself—not at least what you would deem happiness—I only want to recommend the religion I have professed, and be of some little service to those around me. The conviction is ever weighing upon me heavily—more heavily than words can tell—that I do harm instead of good amongst you all. At best I am only a cipher in my own home; I have no influence, and somebody has said that true religion *must* be influential, must diffuse, within a certain radius of itself, a holy atmosphere. Elsie, where is the holiness of this household? where is even the outward harmony? Am I wearying you now, dear, as I weary them all? Ah, I was forgetting that with your hands full of bright flowers— flowers of paradise they appear to you, Elsie— you are not likely to be interested in such sober talk as mine. Kiss me, darling, and then we will each go to our day's work, or—pleasure."

Did it occur to Joanna to contrast *her* work with her little sister's pleasure—to wonder why so much of sunshine was allotted to the one, so much of shadow to the other? Perhaps it did, but if so there was no envy, no bitterness mingling in her thoughts on the subject; nothing as far as Elsie was concerned but an earnest, earnest hope that the happiness she anticipated might not be prejudicial to her higher interests; might not be the means of numbering her with those who have their portion in this world, and to whom at the last it should be said—" Son " or " daughter, remember that thou in thy life time hadst thy good things."

Perhaps, when Joanna shall have talked a little more to Felix concerning the matter so near to both their hearts, she may be won to think with him that there is no fear of Edgar Carlyon's wife being surfeited with so much of human felicity as is represented by the " good things " of the gospel parable.

CHAPTER XI.

UN ENFANT TERRIBLE !

THE dinner that day went off quite as well as the first which had been given to the two Carlyons had done. Mrs. Vining had recovered her outward equanimity, and was as resplendant in black silk and white streamers as ever. James Oliver was allowed the privilege of leading her into the dining-room, and though this young man was not an especial favorite of the widow's, she did not, on the present occasion, object to be entertained by him, thinking perhaps that if by chance he should take a fancy to her (now that there was no hope for him of Elsie) he would at least be as eligible as the chimney sweeper she had professed herself quite ready to marry in the morning. As poor Lillie had returned a sorrowful negative to the invitation which had again been sent round to her, Master Arthur was once more allowed a place at the table, and this time his mother had his chair close to her own, and gave some personal attention both to the quality and quantity of the food the young gentleman partook of.

"They have frightened me about my dear boy," she said to Mr. Oliver in explanation of the restrictions she was for the first time in her life laying upon the child's appetite—"do *you* think he looks as if there was anything the matter with him?"

James Oliver was naturally very fond of children, and he and Arthur had always been good friends, in spite of the boy's waywardness and disinclination to care for anybody who would not pet and spoil him after his mother's fashion.

"I can't say I think him looking well, Mrs.

Vining," was the candid reply to the question asked—" but children of Arthur's age easily get out of health and almost as easily get in again. I am sure there is nothing for you to be anxious about—only let him eat moderately and take more exercise: he is stout, you see, and has a very brilliant colour."

James Oliver spoke exactly as he thought —and as he had often thought—about Mrs. Vining's child; but in truth he was not paying particular attention (as far as real interest went) either to the son or to the mother to-day. Notwithstanding his earnest efforts to prevent it, his eyes would keep wandering to the opposite side of the table, where Elsie and her lover sat, " he, earth's happiest son, and she her loveliest daughter." It was wonderfully stupid of him— a grave sensible man like James Oliver—but he really could not help repeating that line, out of the song he had last heard Elsie sing, over and over again, as he furtively watched the two, and wondered (with rather more bitterness I am afraid than Joanna Paget had mingled in her train of thought on nearly the same subject) why so full and overflowing a measure of human bliss should be allotted to some men, so poor and scanty a portion to others.

Felix took a little more trouble to make himself agreeable to-day than it was his wont to do. He was gratified at having his friend and partner at table, and he judged also that in Mr. Paget's disturbed state of mind concerning business matters he might be glad of more active assistance than he usually got in entertaining his guests. Not that any casual observer could have discovered the least trace of anxiety beneath the cheerful-looking, gracious, admirably painted mask, which the head of the family had assumed for this occasion—but then his son, being behind the scenes, knew that it *was* a mask, and played his own part accordingly.

Joanna was the only one who might be said to contribute nothing to the general sociability of those assembled for that brief space of time together. She had none of the graces or accomplishments that qualify a woman for shining in society, and the circumstances of her life acting upon and increasing the somewhat morbid tendencies of her mind, she was fast acquiring that outward gloom and joylessness which, above all things, professors of the religion whose ways are ways of pleasantness should endeavour to shun.

Mr. Carlyon, the elder, had sought more than once, out of simple courtesy, to draw this silent, unattractive girl into conversation, but Joanna knew nothing of new operas or exhibitions, cared little for old paintings or modern sculpture, and in short failed utterly in getting up even a semblance of interest in any one of the many topics on which the really good-natured old gentleman tried her.

" She is a fool, without even a fool's capacity for enjoyment," he said to himself at last, when his patience was quite exhausted : and then he turned to Mrs. Paget and extracted some amusement from that lady's pomposity and carefully arranged sentences until she retired, with her three fair daughters and grandson, from the table.

Felix made, soon after, an excuse for drawing Mr. Oliver into the garden. Edgar at the same time joined the drawing-room party, and thus the two fathers were left to enjoy their claret and their private talk alone.

They came in very late, only just before ten o'clock, and when everybody, except the lovers, had grown very tired, and had been thinking the evening would never end. Elsie had sung a little—not " Fairy bells" though, this time—Mrs. Vining had sung and played a great deal; Felix had actually talked for a good half hour with Edgar Carlyon, and Joanna, during an equally prolonged period, with James Oliver. Mrs. Paget had dozed in her comfortable chair, and woke up to snap at Arthur, who had trodden, mischievously, she said, on her toes. And now Joanna had possessed herself of the little torment, and, when her father and Mr. Carlyon came in from the dining-room was persuading

Mrs. Vining to let her take him to bed.   But the young rebel had set up a shrill scream at the proposition, and the weak, fond mother had not the heart to insist upon his obedience.   Mr. Paget was looking both flushed and ill at ease—not at all in the mood to endure a spoiled child's demonstrative waywardness.

"Take him off to bed at once," he thundered, in a voice that rang through the room; "and let this be the last time I ever see him up at ten o'clock at night."

It is a commonly received fact that the sudden anger of a usually even-tempered person affects those against whom it is directed far more than an equal amount of irritability on the part of one who is accustomed to indulge in violence.   Mr. Paget was wont to be rather mild and cheery and complacent in his own family, never interfering in the quarrels between the women, and generally bringing with him an atmosphere that might pass at least for capital stage sunshine.   His present outburst came as a surprise on everybody in the room, and Mrs. Vining, who was only valiant where her own sex was concerned, actually quailed and trembled at her father's voice, and instead of quietly leading the offender away, ran into the second drawing-room and sheltered herself under the wing of the lovers, who had again retired, to whisper and talk nonsense together, there.

So to poor Joanna was left the unenviable task of enforcing the young culprit's obedience, and very indifferently she would have managed it— having in point of fact far less physical strength than her nephew—had not James Oliver kindly come to the rescue. Between them they got him at last outside the door; and then, in spite of his kicks and cries, the gentleman, following Joanna's directions, carried him forcibly up the stairs, she walking close behind, and doing her best to imprison the fighting little hands which were struggling to express on his captor's back and shoulders their keen sense of the indignity to which their owner was thus subjected.

"I hate you both!" he exclaimed, stamping

and sobbing passionately the moment he was safely landed on the nursery floor. "You're a horrid man, without any money but what you earn selling medicines, and aunt Joanna's a nasty ugly old maid. Nobody will ever marry her—mamma says so, and I'm glad of it. I hate—hate—hate you both—I do."

Poor aunt Joanna! she certainly looked neither ugly nor old in the rich mantling crimson that dyed her face and neck as her spoiled little nephew thus rudely insulted the friend she valued so highly.   What *she* was called mattered not a bit—it was by no means the first time that similar epithets had been applied to her—but that Mr. Oliver should be led into the belief that any one in her family was in the habit of speaking contemptuously of him—of mocking at his comparative poverty—this was a grief and a shame that Joanna Paget knew not how to bear.

He, seeing her confusion and distress—rightly deeming it was for him and not for herself she suffered, went up to her kindly and soothingly, and—thinking no more of Arthur—laid his hand somewhat tenderly —for he really felt as a brother towards this poor girl—on hers.

"There is nothing in this to vex you," he said in a low voice. "Who would notice for a moment the wayward expressions of an angry child? Come, we will laugh over our respective descriptions— you cannot say you have been more complimented than myself. Let me see—"

"Oh, you had better kiss her at once," screamed the small madman at this point, "she would like nothing better, ugly old maid as she is! I know she's in love with you, or she wouldn't always get so red when you speak to her. Do marry her, *do*, for you are both nasty and horrid and cross, and I hate you both."

It would be difficult to decide which of the two, standing in such friendly proximity when Master Vining began speaking, moved the quickest from the other, or exhibited the most profound embarrassment when that young gentleman's impertinence had reached its climax. Joanna covered her burning face for a minute, and something like a stifled sob fell upon Mr. Oliver's ear, but he dared not attempt to comfort her now; a barrier, raised indeed by little foolish, childish hands, but a mighty barrier notwithstanding, had suddenly arisen between them, and might possibly never more be thrown down. Happily for them both the servant whom the nursery bell had summoned came in quickly at this most awkward moment, and, taking possession of the delinquent left them free to separate, and recover their composure as best they could.

"I hate you both, you know," reiterated the amiable cause of all this pain and shame and annoyance, as they moved at very respectful distances in the direction of the door, "and I never want either of you to come near me again!"

Poor little ignorant, heedless boy! He could not guess under what circumstances—new and strange and unwelcome to himself—he should soon be brought to reverse these passionate words.

CHAPTER XII

THE WILMOTS IN HOT WATER

FELIX and his father had a very few words together the next morning on the subject of the latter's difficulties. He told his son that Mr. Carlyon would help him through, in consideration of the pending union between their children, but that he had joined to his concession so much outspoken advice as to the future, that Mr. Paget could not but deem he was receiving the obligation under rather arbitrary conditions. Mr. Carlyon ventured to think that his old friend was keeping up an establishment beyond his means, and suffering extravagancies in his household which it would henceforth be his duty—at any rate until fortune smiled upon him again—to check. Very evident it was that Mr. Paget had not at all relished the lecturing and the counsel which had followed upon the exposure of his pecuniary embarrassments to Edgar's father.

"Hang it!" he said in giving Felix a very slight sketch of what had passed, " if it were not for the women I would a thousand times rather throw the whole thing up, and begin life over again, than lay myself under an obligation to a man who believes he knows better than the whole world put together; but these women, Felix—why, if I only suggested dismissing a single female servant, wouldn't all Bayswater be raised?"

"And what," asked Felix, " are the especial extravagancies to which Mr. Carlyon referred?"

"Oh, he thought we kept too many servants, gave too many parties in the winter, made too great a show, in fact, altogether. He even wondered why Mrs. Vining did not try to do something for herself and her boy, on being left a widow, rather than come back here to increase the family expenditure. I am sure he cannot wish her comfortably settled elsewhere more heartily than I do, but—"

"But," interrupted Felix hotly, "this is no concern of Mr. Carlyon's, and I in your place should have shown him that I considered his interference the height of impertinence. Surely you did so, sir?"

"You forget," said Mr. Paget, gloomily, "that I was not in a position to speak my mind. We must swallow a vast deal of unpalatable stuff from those whose pockets we are invading. Oh, by the bye, Mr. Carlyon alluded to Elsie's settlements, which he wishes to be of a most liberal and handsome kind, the whole of her own fortune to be secured to her and her children, should there be any, and three thousand a year for life from her husband in the event of her surviving him. He is anxious too to have the wedding hurried on, as he has to be back in Paris, he says, in a month's time, so I have been talking to your mother this morning, and she thinks she can get Elsie's consent to its taking place in about three weeks."

Felix groaned inwardly, but his reason telling him how worse than useless would be any further arguments or representations from himself on the subject, he said not another word but walked round very moodily and discontentedly to the surgery.

Early in that afternoon a little twisted note, written hurriedly in pencil, and not even sealed, was brought to him by his sister Lillie's servant.

It contained only these words.

"Come to me for half an hour as soon as you possibly can. Dick is out now, but may be home any moment. Don't say a word at the house about my having sent for you.

"Yours,

"Lillie."

As this missive happened to arrive just before

Dr. Paget was starting on his afternoon rounds, and he had a patient or two in the direction of Paddington, it was quite convenient to him to attend to poor Lillie's summons at once.

" Something wrong there again, no doubt," was the not very cheering thought with which he went on his way ; and this thought became a certainty the moment the house door was opened to him, and his sister, with flushed cheeks and excited manner, met him in the passage and drew him hastily into the little parlour before described.

" Felix," she said, " it's all up with us at last. Dick has received his dismissal from the office this morning ; we are over head and ears in debt, and everything we have in the world will now be seized and sold. I know you can't do anything to help us, and that my father won't ; but I thought it best to tell you how things stand, because there is no saying what may happen from one moment to another. When Dick came home with the news, he had already been drinking heavily, and now he has gone out again, taking with him all the money we had in the house. I have not even a brass farthing left," she continued, with a sudden return to her usual recklessness, and dangling an empty purse in the air as she spoke, "and we have had no dinner to-day, for the butcher sent me a most impertinent message, refusing to give another ounce of meat till his bill was paid. Oh, I am not hungry, Felix," (rightly interpreting the look of acute pain and indignation on her brother's face)—I could not touch the greatest delicacies in London to-day, if they were placed before me; but I am thinking of poor stupid Dick, and wondering what mischief he will be up to now. He really looked desperate when he went out."

"Lillie," said Felix, compelling her to sit down, and then taking a chair beside her, "you must allow me to send your servant for some food for you and for herself. I am a doctor, you know, and must have my way, and then I will talk to you about this sad matter. Have you any wine in the house?"

"A little, I think; but don't force me to drink it, Felix dear. If you only knew how I hate wine, and everything of that sort, which deadens sensation for a while, only to render it ten times more acute afterwards, you would not urge me to take it. I am far stronger than you suppose, both in mind and body."

"But not strong enough, my dear, for the trials you may have to encounter, if you refuse to adopt common precautions in keeping up this strength you boast of. What can you eat, Lillie?'

Poor Lillie shuddered and made a little piteous face of disgust at the very thought of eating. Nevertheless, in this her brother gained his point, and when the light food was nicely cooked and placed before her, she found it quite possible to take sufficient of it to sustain nature, and to assist in modifying that dangerous mental excitement which Felix justly apprehended for her under the circumstances by which she was so unhappily surrounded.

"And now, Lillie," he said, when the tray had been sent away, and he saw that his sister's whole manner was calmer and more natural, "we will go a little more fully into your husband's affairs. Tell me first of all how much you suppose he owes in the neighbourhood."

"Oh," replied Lillie, "I know nothing whatever of his private debts, beyond suspecting them to be considerable. But for household expenses, including wine and spirits, I am sure we must owe above seventy pounds, and I don't believe the whole of our furniture is worth so much as that."

"And if this seventy pounds was paid, Lillie, I am afraid the advantage to you would be very slight indeed, while Mr. Richard Wilmot remains out of a situation."

"The only advantage would be that I might keep a house over my head a little longer, and sometimes I have thought I might try to get lodgers, or even a pupil or two. I am young and strong, you see, Felix, and should be glad enough to work for myself; but while Dick goes on in his present reckless way, what's the good? Ruin *must* come sooner or later."

Yes, that was clear, at any rate, even to the very feeblest intelligence. Nothing but ruin both to husband and wife could result from courses such as those which Mr. Richard Wilmot was pursuing. There was but one remedy, as far as Lillie was concerned, and this, for more reasons than appeared on the surface, Felix Paget shrank from naming.

Nevertheless, the case appeared too urgent to permit of any ordinary scruples, and, after contemplating his sister without speaking for a minute or two, Felix said rather abruptly —

" Lillie, if you choose to leave your husband until *he* chooses to behave differently—at the least to earn for you the means of living respectably, I will give up my present quarters, and make a home for you. I have often thought of doing it for Joanna, who is not as happy as she might be; but you could both come, and I have no doubt whatever of being able to earn enough for us all."

As soon as Lillie's somewhat bewildered mind took in the full sense of her brother's meaning, she shook her head with a look of very steadfast determination.

"Felix, I know how to appreciate the kindness and generosity of this offer on your part; but even in making it you feel, I am certain, that I could not, that I ought not, for a moment to entertain it. I don't speak as poor Joanna would, of the sin against God I should be committing in abandoning my husband, though I suppose it would be that too; but I should feel I was doing a grievous wrong to myself, to my woman's nature, which *must* possess some hidden, but all-sufficient strength, to fight out the battle of life that nobody else can fight for me. Felix, I don't believe Dick has a spark of true affection left for me, if, indeed, he ever had one, but he has some shadow of respect for the wife who does not fear him, even when he is most violent, and who will not suffer him to drag her down a single inch towards the depths of degradation and sensuality to which he knows too well he is himself rapidly falling. I have no heroic or enthusiastic hopes of converting my husband, Felix; but by staying with him, and sharing as well as I am able all the evil he brings upon himself, 1 may help to preserve him from the worst that might happen to such a man. I may," lowering her voice to a whisper, " keep him at least from crime."

Felix was deeply affected, as who would not have been to have heard this weak and cruelly injured woman thus assert her firm resolve to be true to her marriage vows, and to stand to the very last by the husband she had taken for better or for worse, and who had already proved that the " worse " in its very broadest sense was what alone she had to expect in connection with him.

When Dr. Paget could speak, he said—

" Lillie, my dear, I dare not tell you you are wrong, and I will not tell you now how very earnestly I admire your courage and sense of duty.   I have already outstayed my time, and I want still to settle a little matter of business with you.   You must permit me to send you a cheque for yourself, Lillie, out of which I should wish you to pay enough to your tradespeople here to keep them quiet and ensure their attending to your orders for the next few weeks at any rate.   With the remainder of the money you must buy yourself something nice and pretty to appear in at Elsie's wedding, which is to take place, I regret to say, almost immediately."

" Oh, Felix," exclaimed Lillie, a tear for the first time since he had been with her starting to her eye; " what a contrast between my destiny, in all its miserable reality at this present moment, and Elsie's in all its brilliant promise as to the future! God grant, poor child! that the sunshine may never go down for her as it has done for me."

" Yes, God grant it, Lillie," returned Felix,

solemnly, " but don't let us make too sure that it will be so.   Elsie is not fitted to endure as you are, and a very few storms would crush and beat her to the earth.   I will try and see you to-morrow, Lillie."

" Oh, and I have not thanked you yet for all your goodness to me," said his sister, warmly, as she pressed the hands he extended to her gratefully and lovingly in her own.   " I must accept your bounty for the moment, Felix, but if ever I can work for myself it shall be duly and thankfully repaid.   Hark, there is a step outside, and that is Dick's knock I am certain.   Don't say I sent for you, and, unless he tells you himself what has happened, know nothing—you understand ?"

It proved that Mr. Richard Wilmot was not in a state to tell anything.   How he found his own door was a mystery which only persons of his peculiar habits would be likely to solve.   He staggered through the narrow passage and into the room where his wife and brother-in-law waited for him ; and after a vacant stare at them both he threw himself heavily on the sofa, called, in a scarcely intelligible voice for something to cover him; and in three minutes gave very audible indications of being sound asleep.

Then Felix, not trusting himself to make a single comment, kissed his pale sister, and left her.

CHAPTER XIII.

A MATRIMONIAL TÊTE-À-TÊTE.

AFTER her brother had gone, Mrs. Richard Wil‑ mot—without casting a glance at the prostrate form of her tipsy husband—took out her writing case, and scribbled off a note to the butcher and another to the baker, telling them that a portion of their accounts would be paid to them the following day, and ordering enough meat and bread for present consumption. She knew that her lord and master (such a master!) would awake up both hungry and cross, and that his full fury would be spent on her if she had not a

comfortable and relishing tea prepared and waiting for him.

After this, she took up a book—one of poor
Lillie's chief weaknesses had always been an in-
ordinate passion for novel reading—and for a
little while really succeeded in forgetting her
own actual and present trials in the imaginary
ones of the heroine who sighed and suffered—
principally' in a white muslin dress—through
three thick volumes.

About six o'clock Mr. Richard Wilmot suddenly opened his eyes, yawned in very manly
fashion, stretched his legs till the frail sofa
creaked and groaned under him, and at last called
imperiously to his wife to come and help him into
a sitting posture.

"I'm so confoundedly stiff," he said, "from
all the running about I've had to-day, that I can
scarcely move. I'm precious hungry, too, I can
tell you. What is there for tea, Lillie?"

"There is a mutton-chop and some kidneys for
you," she replied, with her eyes still upon her

book; "when you are ready I will ring for it to be brought up."

"I'm ready now, then, young woman," he said, in the manner and with the accent of a savage addressing his squaw; "and if you don't come and help me up at once, I'll pitch this horsehair cushion at your head. I'm just in the humour for it."

Which Lillie so entirely believed, that she thought it wise to obey, though the shrinking horror she had of approaching her husband, while even the remains of intoxication were discernible in him, was one which, with all her bravery, she had never been able to overcome.

Having seen him safe on his legs, and ascertained that he could walk steadily, the wife returned to her novel—not at all out of bravado, or because she had any wish further to incense Mr. Richard, but simply that she had arrived at a thrillingly interesting chapter, and was impatient to know how the exciting scene on hand would terminate.

"You put that down instanter," cried her amiable helpmate, as he remarked probably the absorbed expression of her countenance; "a pretty wife you are, ain't you, for a man harassed with business and crushed by injustice to come home to! a miserable, lazy reader of dirty, sentimental novels, instead of an intelligent and cheerful companion. Come, miss, shut it up, and fling it out of sight this very minute, and talk to a fellow, can't you. We've got all sorts of pleasant things to talk about, you know, and it would be a pity if we did not take advantage of it. Have you rung the bell?"

"Yes," said Lillie, closing her book with a weary sigh, and putting it in the drawer of the table; "and I am quite ready to talk, Dick, if you'll start a subject. You see more of the world than I do."

"Oh yes, to be sure I do," he sneered; "and a very pretty world it is—for those who've got plenty of money and nothing to do but amuse themselves. I say, Lillie, when is this fine wedding in your family coming off? or has the lover been unlucky enough to discover in time what a nest of hornets he was thinking of connecting himself with? By Jove! I wish *I'd* known something of them before I married you, my girl. Why, that old father of yours wouldn't help a poor wretch to a five-pound note, if he was starving."

"I hope you have not been rash enough to try him again, Dick," spoke out Lillie quickly and apprehensively. "I had trusted we might manage to keep my father and mother from even hearing of our present trouble until you had got another situation. They have already suffered quite enough through me. You have not written to my father, have you ?"

"Why no," he said coolly, "I have had too many of my former letters treated with disdain; but I just looked in upon the old gentleman at his office this morning, and paid him the compliment of explaining my position. I regret to add he had the bad taste to get excited over my communication, and to tell me, in anything but refined language, that if he had thousands to spare, I should not see one penny of it. A nice father-in-law, isn't he ?"

"I am sure you cannot wonder at it, Dick," returned Lillie, deeply mortified at what she heard. "In the first place, my father is really not well off, considering the appearances he must keep up, and the many people he has to support; and in the next place it is such a thankless thing to go on helping a man like you, who will do nothing to help himself."

"Come, none of your abuse or preaching, young woman, if you please. This isn't the sort of conversation I want to hold with you. I want to know whether that fellow, Carlyon, is still fool enough to go on courting Elsie, and if so, when the wedding is to take place ?"

"Here comes Patty with the tea," said Lillie, who had her own reasons for not wishing to answer the inquiry just made, " I am sure you must be hungry, Richard, and I think the chops are nice ones."

Which fortunately proved to be the case. So very nice, indeed, they were, that Mr. Wilmot, having consumed the first dishful, rang and ordered a fresh supply. In the interest and amusement of eating and drinking—the wife had taken care that the tea should be extra strong and extra sweet to-night—this amiable husband suspended his efforts to make himself as disagreeable as possible, and it was only when he had outraged nature to the very utmost of his capacity, and the empty dishes were taken out of his sight, that he remembered where the conversation had broken off, and repeated the question that Lillie had so strong a disinclination to answer.

" Come now, old woman," (You see he was in a little better temper by this time.) " You haven't told me yet when the wedding is to be; and I am just in the humour for listening to agreeable gossip. Besides, I really happen to have an especial interest in this matter. When is it to be?"

Lillie had no choice, thus commanded, but to tell her husband that she believed her sister would be married in a few weeks, upon which Mr. Richard got up from his chair, snapped his fingers, chuckled loudly, and otherwise expressed his very keen satisfaction at the intelligence.

"In a few weeks? That's fine; that will do; that suits me capitally. Now, Lillie, my woman, you must manage to get me invited to the wedding. I don't mean to witness the foolish ceremony. I had enough and to spare of that when I led *you* to the hymeneal, under a temporary aberration of intellect, as the newspapers say— but to the breakfast, you understand, where I can be properly and formally introduced to my new brother-in-law. A marriage in a family, especially such a catch as this, is the very time of all others for making up family quarrels, forgetting old differences, and so forth. I'm under no obligation to your paternal relative at present—in fact, after our meeting of this morning, I may say quite the reverse, therefore I have no objection to be the first to hold out the hand of reconciliation and forgiveness. I shall even feel a satisfaction in showing the old curmudgeon what a good-hearted, noble-minded fellow I can be when I like. Of course, Lillie, you can put all this in any terms you please. I don't care a brass farthing how you do it, as long as you get me the invitation."

Now besides Lillie's own firm conviction of the inexpediency of making her reckless husband known to Edward Carlyon, and her doubts as to her capability of effecting the reconciliation Mr. Richard so suddenly craved, she knew quite well how sensitively and nervously Elsie shrank from the thought of even a chance meeting between the elegant and fastidious gentleman she was to marry, and the coarse ill-mannered Dick Wilmot. Hitherto it had appeared as if there would be no difficulty whatever in keeping them apart, as Mr. Wilmot, since his quarrel with his wife's family, had never once set his foot within the house at Bayswater, and Lillie had believed that nothing short of absolute force would have prevailed to make him do so. Assuredly, the idea of his wishing to attend her sister's wedding breakfast, had never glanced across her mind as the barest possibility. She heard it now with a terror and a distress it was very difficult for her to conceal from her keen-eyed husband. Her voice was far from steady as she replied to his somewhat lengthy harangue.

"I am not at all certain, Richard, of being able to do what you ask. My father is not likely to be better pleased with you on account of your revelations of this morning, and you know that the original quarrel was as much your own as was the occasion of it. Indeed, not to mince matters, or to deceive you," she added, with that sudden courage which is often born of extreme apprehension for others, "I am certain they will not invite you to the wedding, and that I should only be exposing myself to humiliation and defeat were I to propose it."

"Very well," he said, speaking calmly, but drawing in his lips in a way peculiar to himself, when he meant to express one of his obstinate resolves, "then of course they will be prepared to resign the pleasure of your society also, for, by the heavens above us, Lillie," (and here he grew disagreeably white, and struck the table a ringing blow with his clenched hand) "my wife goes to no house from which her husband is excluded, neither then, nor at any future time—do you perfectly understand?"

No doubt poor Lillie did perfectly understand; but her heart was full now, and, too proud to shed tears in the presence of her tyrant, she sat before him silent, and with dry, cold eyes, that looked straight on at the opposite wall, beyond the man who was torturing her.

"Oh, sulky, are you?" he said presently with a coarse laugh. "As if I cared one *iota* for that, or for any other tempers you may think proper to exhibit, young woman. . But come, I don't want to quarrel with you, as long as you behave decently, and take my part, as a good wife should, against that stuck-up family of yours. We will waive the subject of the breakfast for the moment, and you shall tell me something of the plans of the happy pair afterwards. Where are they to live, Lillie?"

This was so direct a question that the wife knew Mr. Dick meant getting a direct answer.

" In Paris, at first, I believe," she replied, very coldly, and with no withdrawal of her eyes from the blank wall.

" At Paris," repeated the gentleman, in quite a cheerful voice. " Well, I admire their taste beyond everything. Paris is a capital *locale* for rich folks, and in my idea a far better one than London for poor ones. Do you know, Lillie, by a curious coincidence I was this very day given the chance of a clerkship in Paris in a wine merchant's business, salary only two thousand francs to begin with, but the hope of an increase soon. I laughed at the notion then, and told my friend I thanked him for nothing; but, by Jove! I'll go the first thing to-morrow and see about it. Paris, without a single acquaintance there, is one-thing, and Paris with a millionaire for a brother-in-law as close to you as you choose to settle yourself, is another. Lillie, my girl, our fortune's made. I see more gold than I can count falling in showers around me. No more grinding at heavy book keeping in dingy London offices, no more snubbing from insolent superiors because a fellow's watch may not always be set to Greenwich mean time, nor his hand quite so steady in the mornings as it was while he remained a school-boy. We'll away to sunny France, my woman, and you shall be dressed in silk and feathers like the finest of them, and we'll lead a regular jolly life and enjoy ourselves. Ha, ha, ha! what a capital idea this is, and all on two thousand francs, a little less than eighty pounds, a year! But I'm clever, I'm sharp, I'm a gentleman of endless resources you see. Now ring for Patty, my dear, and we'll send her for a bottle of champagne. Look, I've half a sovereign left, and I'll pay for it like a man—a bottle of champagne, Lillie, to drink success to our new enterprise. Come, don't go on staring at vacancy, but give your orders to that slow footed damsel of yours, and you shall have a fair share, when it comes, of your favourite wine."

But Lillie did not stir to ring the bell; and when Patty appeared in answer to her master's loud summons Mrs. Wilmot only said, in a singularly hard and constrained voice,

"Bring me my bed room candle; and after that you can shut up the house."

When the candle was brought the wife took it and left the room without a word.

Then Mr. Richard, feeling that it was a lost game as far as the jolly evening he had contemplated was concerned, kicked off his boots, returned the half sovereign to his waistcoat pocket, lighted a very dirty meerschaum pipe and threw himself on the creaking sofa again, to smoke and ruminate at his ease.

An hour later, when Patty had followed her mistress's example and gone to bed, the master of the house found his way to the larder, took out all the cold meat it contained, and, with the addition of bread and cheese and ale, made a very excellent meal by the remnant of the kitchen fire.

This over, he too dragged himself to bed, and no doubt dreamt, beside his sleepless wife, of that golden shower of fortune which was to descend upon him as soon as his intrinsic worth should become known to his new brother-in-law.

CHAPTER XIV.

LILLIE'S TWO VISITORS.

FELIX was unable to see his sister the next day, but he sent her the promised cheque with a very affectionate note, bidding her keep up her spirits, take especial care of her own health, and hope for brighter times. Poor Lillie, who was still smarting under the bitter annoyance of the previous evening, sighed drearily as she read this brotherly epistle, and thought that the only brighter times she could reasonably look forward to were those which should follow the putting on of her grave clothes, unless it chanced that Richard Wilmot underwent that ceremony before her. And if bad husbands are shocked that wives should ever contemplate with anything less than horror and despair the idea of their demise, they must remember that the thirst for happiness and peace is too strong a principle in the human heart, for a woman—more especially a young one—voluntarily to relinquish all hope of these blessings, and sit down with meekly folded hands under the dominion of a selfish tyrant.

Lillie Wilmot, as I have endeavoured to show, was as brave and uncomplaining under her trials as any woman, unaided by Divine grace, could be, and she had resolved to do what she believed to be her duty by this unworthy husband of hers, to the very last; but I cannot affirm that his death would, at that time, have had a particularly crushing effect upon her, or that the prospect of a long life shared with him was otherwise than odious and repugnant to her every thought.

On the Sunday of that week, after morning

church, Mrs. Vining, as was occasionally her habit when she had no other visit to make, walked over to Paddington to call upon her married sister. It was known in the family now that Mr. Richard Wilmot was out of a situation again, and while they all compassionated poor Lillie sincerely, they nearly all blamed her for not separating herself from him, and leaving such a ne'er-do-well to his fate. Amongst those who railed at the wife's stupidity Mrs. Vining was foremost, and she had come quite prepared to give her sister a piece of her mind on the subject.

"Missis is laying down on her bed with a headache," said Patty, as soon as she recognised the owner of the black crape and white streamers, "and master's having lunch in the parlour with a gentleman he brought home with him an hour ago. Will you be shown in there, ma'am, please, or up to missis?"

"Up to your mistress, by all means," replied Georgina Vining, with a gesture of disgust, as the fumes of bad spirits and worse tobacco were wafted to her through the chinks of the parlour door;" and you need not tell Mr. Wilmot that I am here."

Poor Lillie raised her throbbing head with difficulty from the pillow, as her sister's rustling silks became audible in her room.

" Oh, is it you, Georgina?" she said wearily, " I scarcely expected you to-day, as it is so late. How are they all at home? "

"Pretty well, I fancy; but pray lay your head down again, my poor child, and don't attempt to talk yet. You look ghastly, and no wonder! *I* shall talk to *you*."

" Do," said Lillie, rather faintly ; " I want to hear about Elsie and her wedding. Make yourself comfortable, Georgina, and let Patty bring you a glass of wine."

" No, not a thing," Mrs. Vining answered decidedly. " I took my luncheon before I left home; that made me later than usual; and I also waited a short time for Joanna, who has been detained, I suppose, by some of her almshouse people, and will follow me here. She wants to see you, too."

"Ah," sighed Lillie from her pillow, "you are all very kind. Dick says, now, I am never to come near any of you again—never to come to Bayswater—I mean. He wanted me to get him an invitation to the wedding, and when I told him I knew it could not be done, he swore I should not go to it either, nor go any more at all to a house from which he was banished. You must explain this to mamma and little Elsie. I am sorry, very sorry, not to see her married, but it can't be helped."

"But it *shall* be helped, Lillie!" exclaimed the widow excitedly; "why I never heard of such a thing in the whole course of my life!—not have you at the wedding, your own sister's wedding, the last there will ever be in the family, too!— the idea is preposterous, absurd. We were talking it over last night at home, and Felix said *he* would see that you had the means of getting a suitable dress for the occasion, and mamma (who, by the bye, pretends to be excessively straitened for money just now), said she was sorry not to be able to help you; but she has sent you a couple of sovereigns just for your own present use, Lillie: here, you had better put them away before Dick can get at them. If you will persist in remaining with such a brute, you must consent to deceive him sometimes."

On this point, Lillie's conscience was sufficiently elastic. She had been obliged to pay away nearly every penny she had received from her brother, and it was with a feeling of extreme thankfulness, even in the midst of the heavy grief that weighed upon her just now, that she took her mother's timely gift and deposited it safely in the same old purse which, a few days before, she had laughingly exhibited in its empty condition, to Felix.

" I wish *I* was in circumstances to assist you also," said Mrs. Vining, with perfect sincerity; " but I need not tell you, Lillie, that I am poorer than yourself, and with a child dependent on me.

I am thinking seriously of going out as house-keeper to an elderly gentleman, and only hesitate because I don't know how my darling Arthur would get on without me."

" Oh, if we were richer, and I might have Arthur, how happy it would make me!" exclaimed poor Lillie, with sudden animation, " but with the certainty of being constantly in hot water, constantly on the verge of starvation, I dare not offer to take him, even if Dick would allow me."

" What does your beautiful husband propose doing?" asked Georgina Vining, who had in reality about as much thought of attempting an arctic expedition as she had of working for her own livelihood or giving up her son. " Has he any occupation at all in view?"

" I know nothing of his plans," said Lillie, " for we are not on the most friendly terms just now. I believe he is looking out for a situation; but without a recommendation from his last employers, I don't think he can have much chance."

Mrs. Wilmot did not consider it desirable to mention to her gossipping sister what Mr. Richard had hinted about going to Paris. In the first place, he had not alluded to the subject since that night, and in the next place, she felt sure the very suggestion of such a thing would annoy and frighten Elsie, and set the whole family ten times more than ever against her husband. Poor Lillie was still girl enough to desire very earnestly to be one of the guests at her sister's wedding, and she knew that there would remain no shadow of a hope for her, if, by unveiling Mr. Wilmot's motives for wishing himself to be of the party, she provided her parents with an unanswerable excuse for excluding him from it.

She meant to tell everything to Felix the next time he came to see her, but then he was a man, and his discretion, as well as his judgment, could be relied on. Georgina Vining, without intending to make mischief, would be sure to chatter at home of any and everything she discovered at the Wilmots, and so Lillie, in this matter, kept her own counsel, and claimed no sympathy as regarded the very heaviest of the burdens which were just then weighing so cruelly upon her.

" It is no use my staying this morning," Mrs. Vining said presently. " I am only making your head worse, and I promised Arthur a walk in Kensington Gardens. You will be having Joanna here directly, and I have no doubt she will preach you a sermon of an hour's length, as it is Sunday, and you haven't been to church. Good bye, Lillie. Keep up your spirits, if you can, and give it that man well if he teazes you.   I would, I know, if he were mine. I'd punch his head against the wall till he shouldn't be able to swear whether it was his own or somebody else's. By the bye, Lillie, I suppose we must manage to have him at the breakfast. I think they would all rather endure this than lose you. I will talk it over with Elsie and Mamma, and write you a line to-morrow. Tuesday fortnight is fixed for the ceremony."

Then this voluble lady kissed her sister's pale

cheek and took herself and her rustling silks out of sight and hearing. The atmosphere of Lillie Wilmot's darkened room was anything but cheering to-day, and Mrs. Vining felt that she should need all the sunshine of the gardens, with the pleasing excitement of watching Arthur feed the swans, and observing the interest her pretty boy awakened in the idlers round the water, before the gloom that had settled on her spirits could be dissipated.

Lillie, left to herself, managed to sleep for about half-an-hour, and when she opened her eyes again, with her head in some degree relieved, it was to find her sister Joanna sitting in her quaker-like costume and with her grave sad face turned towards the bed, beside her.

"Lillie dear, I am so glad you have been sleeping. Patty told me you had a headache, and that Georgina had only just left you. I came up very quietly and should have gone without disturbing you if you had not awakened soon. Are you any better?"

" Yes, thank you, Jo, and glad to see you here. I will get up now, and we will have the window open, and let in the fresh air and the sunshine. It seems a lovely day.   You came alone, I suppose?"

" Yes.   Felix would have been glad to come with me; he bade me tell you so with his love; but he and Mr. Oliver have had scarcely a moment they can call their own these last few days.   The scarlet fever is raging all about the neighbourhood, and doctors are in extraordinary request.   Numbers of children have already died of the disease, and Felix thinks it is increasing rather than diminishing."

" Isn't Georgina in a way about Arthur?" asked Lillie, as she threw open the window, and brought chairs for Joanna and herself on either side of it.   " I wonder she did not speak of it here."

" She knows nothing about it," Joanna replied, " and we are most anxious that she should not. She would frighten herself into a nervous fever, at the least, and worry Felix to death by sending for him every time Arthur had an ache or a pain of any description. But now to return to your own affairs, dear Lillie. Has Richard succeeded in getting another place yet?"

" Oh no," answered Lillie, half groaning at the thought of having to go through a repetition of her troubles; " it isn't such an easy thing, Joanna; but indeed I am in complete ignorance of his plans. I only know we are deeply in debt, and that if it hadn't been for Felix's kindness we should be starving at the present moment. He lent me enough to pay something to each of the tradespeople upon whom we are most dependent, and so for a little while they have agreed to go on supplying us. By and by, however, the crash *must* come—we shall be sold up, and then goodness only knows what our fate will be."

" Lillie," said Joanna in her slow calm way, " ' I have a little money of my own, saved out of my allowance for clothes. I save a portion every year, that I may have to give to those who need. You need it now, dear, and therefore you must not refuse to take it from me. It is not much—only between nine and ten pounds—but even this little may help you till your husband is employed again; and you may be sure I shall never ask you for it back."

"Oh you dear, dear Jo," cried poor, impulsive Lillie, with tears streaming now from her eyes, "how good and thoughtful and unselfish of you; but you are all so good to me that it breaks my heart, and causes me more suffering than the whole of Dick's tyranny. Put up your purse, my darling, for I will not take it yet; not till I am absolutely in want. Mamma has sent me two sovereigns, and I assure you with this, and what I have left from Felix's money, I feel myself quite a rich lady."

"Well, anyhow, it is yours, Lillie," said Joanna, restoring her purse to her pocket, "and you can claim it whenever you like. Will you accept a little book from me to-day, as you decline the money for the present. I have had it some time, but I should be glad for you to have it now."

It is just possible that had Joanna offered the book before she offered the money, Lillie might have answered ungraciously, that it was no use bringing sermons or tracts to her; but Joanna had too well paved the way for her second gift, to leave her sister any loophole for its non-acceptance; so the small, neatly bound volume was taken with rather a sickly smile, and a "Thank you, dear Jo; I have no doubt it is very nice."

"I think, Lillie, you would at least find more comfort from its perusal than you can find from those novels and romances you spend so much time in reading. Will you try for my sake, dear —to please me."

"Oh, certainly Jo," said poor Lillie, glancing rather ruefully at the title, "but it does not suggest anything very lively or cheering, does it? *The Night of Weeping* is such an ominous name for a book."

"Yet," urged the elder sister, mildly, "when

the night of weeping really comes to us, dear
Lillie, we are glad and thankful to learn how
and where consolation is to be found. Apart from
the Bible itself, I know of no book which speaks
so sweetly and soothingly to those in trouble as
this one, which I am asking you to read. It is
beautifully written, too—a fine poem throughout."

"Well, I will read it this afternoon, Jo, I give
you my word; but please don't abuse my poor
novels. If I were like you, I should naturally
and instinctively prefer more serious works,
and fly to them in my daily troubles and vexa-
tions; but being as I am—of the earth earthy—
I find immense comfort and support—you look
incredulous, but I repeat that I do find support
in my harmless fictions. They take away my
thoughts, for the time being, from myself and
my miserable surroundings; and if I could not
thus get away in spirit from the sad actualities
of my position, substitute occasionally the ideal
for the real, I tell you, Jo, I should either go
mad, or die of a broken heart."

"Well, well," said Joanna, rising and pressing affectionately the hand with which Lillie would have detained her yet a little longer. "I cannot argue this matter with you. I can only ask God to lead you to the true source of comfort and peace, to that source which will never fail or disappoint you, however dark and cold your night of weeping may be. Believe me, Lillie, there will come a time when novels shall have no power to assuage your heartache, when you will crave real help, real support. In that hour I pray that my little book may do its work. And now, dear, good bye."

So poor Lillie was again left alone with her throbbing head, her gloomy thoughts, and her sister Joanna's as yet unvalued gift laying on the chair beside her.

She read it through in the course of the afternoon, because she had promised to do so, but she found it very dull and devoid of interest, and wished that the long Sunday were over, that she might return to more congenial literature.

Mr. Richard paid her a visit when his friend had left him, but what he communicated to her did not tend to brighten her spirits nor to relieve her physical sufferings. He, however, was in one of his least objectionable moods, and as a mark of most unusual favour, he proposed when they had had some tea, that—the evening being fine and mild—his wife should take a walk with him for the benefit of her headache.

" Let us," he said jocosely, as Lillie, in her indifference to everything, assented to his wish, " Let us see what we can of our native country while we remain upon its favoured soil.   Had Britain had the sense to appreciate us more, she need never have lost us.   As it is—"

" I won't walk a step with you," interrupted Lillie decisively, " if you choose as a subject of conversation what you know is hateful to me.   If you must drag me out of my own country to starve or live on charity in a foreign land, at least spare me the anticipation of it.   Mind,

Dick, I will not hear or know beforehand a word of your disgraceful plans."

So Mr. Dick, who probably had his own reasons for not wishing to quarrel just now with his wife, gave up the point, and during their short walk along the Kilburn road, amused himself by whistling popular airs of a not very refined description, and in looking under the bonnets of all the smartly dressed servant girls they happened to meet.

CHATER XV.

MRS. RICHARD WILMOT'S VISIT TO BAYSWATER.

THE result of the family discussion on the subject
of Mr. Richard Wilmot was quite in accordance
with the assurance Mrs. Vining had given to his
wife, namely—an unanimous resolve that it would
be better to put up for a few hours with that
gentleman's obnoxious society than forego the
pleasure of having poor Lillie at Elsie's wedding.
Mr. Paget had certainly remarked that he did
not think he *could* be civil to the man, after the
cool insolence with which Mr. Richard had treated
him at their last meeting, but Mrs. Paget came
to the rescue by deciding that there would be no

necessity to be civil to him, as long as plenty to eat and drink was placed before him. And so a formal invitation was written and sent to Paddington, requesting the pleasure of Mr. and Mrs. Wilmot's company on the 15th instant; and Lillie, who had seen none of her own people since the Sunday, and had almost given up hopes of seeing them again, inasmuch as her husband was constantly reiterating his commands that she should not venture to Bayswater, and telling her that in a few weeks they should be over the water— Lillie, in a flutter of rejoicing took the note to Mr. Richard, who spent a good deal of his time at home now, and asked him if she might not go and carry to her mother their acceptance of the invitation that afternoon.

" Well, I don't mind if you do," he said, when he had considered the matter a little—"this is through your diplomacy I suppose, and diplomacy if successful always ought to be rewarded in some way. Find out all you can, however, and don't chatter about our own affairs. As to the situation in Paris, mum's the word, Lillie, or you and I shall fall out. I hope you've got a good dinner for me to-day. When a man's forced to be idle, his appetite is sure to improve."

Which in Mr. Richard's case was scarcely a desideratum. Nevertheless, his wife (who really, poor girl! wanted so little to make her happy) replied cheerfully that she would go and see to that important matter herself; and as she had learned since her marriage to cook very tolerably, especially those dishes which her master loved, she contrived on the present occasion to satisfy him so completely that he laid down to sleep after his abundant meal in quite a good temper, and yielding Lillie the gracious permission to remain with her family the whole afternoon.

What a contrast that bright, sunny, luxuriously furnished drawing-room at Bayswater presented to the small, dingy, littered parlour that Mrs. Wilmot had left behind her. As she opened the door, and took in at a glance the comfort and the elegance and the brightness that the scene

within presented, and saw her sisters, Georgina
and Elsie, sitting in apparent enjoyment on the
soft couches, where the sun's rays fell upon them,
and bathed them in its cheering warmth and
light, she could not help— this hapless Lillie—
breathing a quick sigh of envy, and recalling
with disgust her own home at Paddington, where
gloom and untidiness held their reign undis-
puted, and where the odours of tobacco and spirits
contrasted miserably with the perfume of the
rare hot-house flowers (Edgar's daily gift to his
betrothed), that here literally filled the air with
their delicious and most acceptable fragrancy.

It was well for Richard Wilmot's wife that
she possessed greater warmth of heart than sensitiveness of mind—perhaps, though, had it been
otherwise she might never have married such a
man ; but on the present occasion the fact, as it
stood, enabled poor Lillie very soon to forget the
bitterness of her first emotions on entering the
room which offered so striking a contrast to her
own, in the pleasure she experienced from the

warm and hearty welcome they all gave her. She was most anxious to impress her mother and sisters with the notion that in spite of her recent additional troubles, she was as cheerful and happy as possible; but at the very first words of affectionate greeting addressed to her, this foolish Lillie burst into tears, and it was a long time before she could manage to regain any degree of composure.

"Pray don't cry, my dear child," said Mrs. Paget with some genuine feeling showing itself under her own eyelids, "or we shall all anathematize that bad husband of yours even more than we do at present. Take off your bonnet, Lillie, and Georgina shall fetch you some wine and cake. You must have loads of news to tell us, and Elsie has some very pretty things to show you by and bye. Come now, you are better, my love, and won't cry any more; it makes me so horribly low and nervous."

As soon as she could, Lillie not only checked her tears but apologized for having been so weak and silly as to shed them; she was quite well and jolly, she declared, only she had not been home for such a time, and the sight of them all overcame her, and she was so happy at the thought of coming to the wedding—darling Elsie's wedding. And then there was a sudden and tremendous hugging and kissing between Elsie and herself, during which Hector, who had been asleep at his young mistress's feet, woke up and stretched and yawned in his usual lazy fashion, and stared at Lillie as if she was a stranger for a minute or two, but finally came towards her with a friendly look, and presented his huge paw to be shaken.

And then Lillie was very nearly going off again, so nervous and hysterical had this un-expected treat of coming to Bayswater made her, but mastered herself in time, and sitting down on the sofa beside Elsie asked her quite composedly whatever she would do without Hector, or Hector without her.

" Oh," replied the dog's fair mistress, looking

radiantly happy, as indeed she was, " we shall neither of us be put to so cruel a test. Edgar dislikes dogs himself, but he won't hear of my being parted from Hector; isn't it good and kind of him ?"

" Yes, charming," assented Lillie, whose spirits were rapidly rising, " why isn't he here now, Elsie; will he be coming before I have to leave? I should like to know something more of my future brother."

" I expect him every minute," Elsie blushingly answered, " but he has a great deal to do just now of course, and. so have we—haven't we, mamma? Oh, Lillie, you must come presently and look at my things that are finished, and some others that Edgar and Mr. Carlyon have given me. We have the spare room up-stairs quite full, and there is a dressmaker working in the house all day. I am sure I shall never be able to wear one half of what is being made for me; Lillie, have you thought about your own dress for the fifteenth yet ?"

"No, darling, but I shall now.   There will be lots of time, and Felix has given me the money for it.   Mamma, it is so kind of you"—she added, turning to her mother—"and of papa too, to invite Dick.   I feel I can never thank you enough for it."

Oh, nonsense, child," said Mrs. Paget, " we were not going to do without *you*; and you must try your best to drill him into decent behaviour, Lillie.   It would be dreadful if he were to do anything outrageously vulgar on such an occasion. Edgar is *so* sensitive and refined."

Poor Lillie thought with inward trembling of Dick's expressed intention of establishing himself close to this fastidious and sensitive gentleman ; but she only smiled dubiously now, and said she fervently trusted he would conduct himself properly at the wedding breakfast.

"And, pray," put in Georgina Vining, who had taken no active part in the conversation as yet, being busily engaged in embroidering a magnificent velvet tunic for Arthur—"pray, Lillie, see that Richard is dressed like a gentleman ; don't let him wear checked trowsers and a colored neck tie protruding a quarter of a yard on either side of his ridiculous chin. The Carlyons having lived so much abroad are particularly alive to any absurdities in the way of outward costume. I hope we shall get Joanna to come out a little more stylishly than usual for the wedding. She really wouldn't be bad looking at times if she took pains with her dress, and laid aside those frightfully unbecoming neutral tints. People with indifferent complexions should always have some bright colours about them to set them off. Few can bear either black or grey, alone."

Of course, Mrs. Vining esteemed herself one of these few, or she would certainly have abjured her widow's sombre garments long ago.

"Where is Joanna to-day ?" Lillie asked now, perhaps growing a little tired of hearing her husband's sins and short-comings so freely commented upon.

"Oh, gadding about somewhere," replied

Georgina, testily—"and doing her utmost to catch all sorts of horrid diseases and bring them home to us. As for Felix we see nothing of him at all—he scarcely takes time to eat his dinner even when he comes in to it. He and James Oliver will make a fortune rapidly at this rate."

"Come up now and look at my pretty things, Lillie dear," said Elsie, coaxingly—" I shouldn't be able to show them to you if Edgar arrived, and he is over his time as it is. Mamma will spare you to me for ten minutes."

So the two went up together to the room where Elsie's finery, and such presents as she had already received, were displayed. Nothing could have charmed Lillie more than to examine critically and uninterruptedly these elegant and costly dresses and ornaments, while at the same time she could indulge in the rare luxury of a long private chat with her favorite sister, and gather some details of the courtship which had hitherto revealed itself to her mind and imagination as something more vague and shadowy than the love affairs she daily read about and wept over.

"And is he very, very devoted, and chivalrous, and nice, Elsie, darling?" she asked, as they stood looking at a beautiful set of emeralds, Mr. Edgar's last gift. "Is he anything like Thaddeus of Warsaw, or Quentin Durward, or that delightful and fascinating Colonel Hubert in Widow Barnaby. Do you know, Elsie, I was madly in love with Colonel Hubert when I read that book, and it seemed so cruel to be roused out of a delicious dream, in which I had quite succeeded in fancying myself Agnes Willoughby, by Dick's beginning to snore hideously on the sofa. Oh! Elsie, dearest," she added with a sudden grave and sorrowful earnestness, "I do hope you will continue to be in love with Mr. Carlyon after you are married to him. It is so dreadful to feel anything less than love for the man you have to obey and pass your life with."

"Indeed it must be, my poor darling," assented happy Elsie with a shudder; "but that could never be the case with anybody who had once loved Edgar Carlyon. Oh, Lillie, I don't know whether he is like Thaddeus of Warsaw, or Colonel Hubert, for I have read neither of the books you mention; but I do know that he quite realises my ideal of what a man *should* be to win and retain a woman's devoted affection. I shall love him dearly, dearly, always."

"Elsie," said her sister, rather abruptly, "they talk so much about his fastidiousness and sensitiveness. In what way do these peculiarities manifest themselves?"

"I scarcely know," acknowledged Elsie after a pause—"he certainly never alludes to the possession of such feelings, and yet in some way or other he impresses us all with the conviction that he has them in an uncommon degree. I think one thing is that he never jokes or seems amused at the jokes of other people; that he laughs very little, and that his manner generally has a loftiness and reticence about it that strangers might mistake for pride."

"Perhaps it is pride," observed Lillie with a bluntness which she regretted the next moment when she saw how shocked and hurt her little sister was looking.

"Oh indeed, indeed it is not," the bride elect eagerly exclaimed. "You should have seen him in the park the other day, Lillie, actually carrying a great heavy bundle for a poor man who was walking the same way as ourselves, and groaning under his load. Edgar talked to him as if he recognized no difference in their positions, gave him money, though the man had not begged, and finally carried that unsightly bundle at least half a mile. If he were proud, would he have done this, Lillie, and have done it as though such kindnesses were of every day occurrence with him? I can imagine that he would sternly resent a liberty, and put down, with a single glance, any one who was bold enough to offer it to him ; but this is not pride—only self respect and dignity."

Again poor Lillie thought with a sinking heart of their future home on some fourth or fifth story of a Paris hotel, and saw in imagination her husband in his snobbish costume and with his boisterous and familiar manners, accosting the elegant Mr. Carlyon in the public streets, and taking every shameless advantage of the chance connection between them.

"Perhaps, Elsie," she said, " mamma will not like my staying away from her any longer. I have so enjoyed looking at all these lovely things, and having such a nice gossip with you, dear; but I suppose we must go down now."

And as there came at the same moment a loud peal at the hall bell, which sent the rich blood dancing all over Elsie's face, that young lady made no objection to her sister's proposal, but, on the contrary, ran lightly in advance of her along the passage and down the stairs, arriving at the foot of them just in time to meet her lover and present him gaily to Lillie, saying, "Edgar, my dear sister, Mrs. Wilmot, is anxious to become better acquainted with you."

" The honor and the pleasure will be all mine," replied the gentleman, taking the hand that Lillie frankly extended to him, and, bowing over it rather than shaking it, as she in her warm-heartedness would have deemed it most natural for him to do—"I hope we are to have the happiness of Mrs. Wilmot's society at dinner to-day."

When Lillie replied that, unfortunately, she could not be spared so long from home, Mr. Carlyon seemed to consider that he had done all in the way of friendly advances that politeness and good feeling exacted; and, turning to his beautiful and blushing Elsie, he took her hand with unmistakable tenderness, and led her—Lillie preceding them—into the drawing room.

The remainder of the time that Mrs. Richard Wilmot ventured to linger at Bayswater, flew by only too quickly. Arthur came in from his afternoon walk in the gardens, and was immediately seized upon, and nearly devoured by his loving Aunt Lillie, who, poor as she was, had invested a small sum on her road from Paddington in French *bon-bons*, for her darling nephew. They played together on the lawn for some time, till Joanna, who had returned at last from her wanderings, strolled out to them, and took Lillie aside to tell her there was no abatement of the scarlet fever, and that she herself had been to see one poor family where four children were down at once with it.

"I don't think you do well to go into such houses, Joanna," said Mrs. Wilmot; "especially as there is this child at home here. What does Felix say about it?"

"Felix does not know anything of it," Joanna replied, "and, indeed, this is the first day that my visitings have led me into the fever districts. I am not in the least afraid for myself, but I shall probably not go again. I happened to meet Mr.

Oliver as I left the house, and he said I was wrong to run the risk of infection for Arthur—he spoke so earnestly on the subject that he made me rather nervous about what I had already done. I suppose I must keep at a distance from Arthur for some days."

It struck Lillie that her calm and sober sister manifested a very curious degree of agitation as she gave this very simple recital. It was a perfect mystery to her why Joanna should get red and then white, and speak with quivering lips about a matter of so commonplace a nature. Lillie, of course, did not know that the accidental meeting of to-day between James Oliver and Joanna Paget was the first that had occurred since the evening of Master Arthur's overwhelming observations; and even had she known so much, she would have been no wiser concerning her sister's strange emotions; for, romantic and imaginative as poor Lillie undoubtedly was, it would have been impossible for her to have

imagined anything so wild as a human attachment, especially an unrequited one, on the part
of the cold, and good, and passionless Joanna.

She looked at her sister for a minute or two
without speaking—so full of wonder was she at
that sister's unusual demonstration. Then she
said (adopting in her own mind the only explanation that presented itself), "Oh, I don't
think you could have done much harm in a single
visit, and as you say you can keep at a safe distance from Arthur. If Georgina would spare him,
I should be but too happy to take him home with
me, but I suppose it would be no use asking
her."

"Not the least," responded Joanna, quickly.
"You know she never will have him away from
her for a single day; and I confess myself too
great a coward, Lillie, to tell her what I have
done, as a reason for letting you have him."

"There is no need to tell her anything," assented Mrs. Wilmot; "she would lead you a
dog's life ever after, and if we come to think of it,

why should you bring infection more than Felix, who sees, perhaps, fifty cases a day? Don't trouble yourself further about it, Jo. I shouldn't. Come in now to the breakfast room with me; mamma is going to give me a quiet cup of tea there, before I start for home. Oh, I have so thoroughly enjoyed this visit."

As I have said before, "poor Lillie" really wanted so little to make her happy! But alas! that little was becoming more and more rarely within her reach.

CHAPTER XVI.

THE WEDDING MORNING.

THE fifteenth of October dawned at last, and was marvellously like the few dull, grey, chilly days, that had preceded it. No brilliant sunshine, no impossible azure sky greeted Elsie's eager vision as she sprang from her bed on her wedding morning, and drew aside the window blind to see what the fates had done for her in the way of weather. Apparently they neither had done nor intended to do anything to speak of, in this really interesting matter, and Elsie who, like all young and romantic girls, had ever associated blue skies and glowing sunshine with her marriage day, was conscious of a keen sensation of disappointment, mingled with something that seemed to strike coldly at her heart, as she looked out at the gloomy atmosphere, and failed to detect even the faintest speck of blue peeping hopefully through those leaden clouds that were dense enough to hide any amount of far off brightness.

Hurrying on her clothes (not of course the bridal garments yet) very quietly for fear of disturbing Joanna, Elsie crept downstairs with the intention of taking a solitary turn in the garden, to see if the morning air—fresh and pure as it generally is in October—would remove the weight from her spirits, and help to brace her for the excitements and fatigues of the day.

Just as she had tied on her garden hat, and wrapped a warm shawl round her, Felix appeared on the lawn coming rapidly to the house from his surgery.

"I am glad to find you downstairs, my dear," he said, kissing her and gazing into her sweet face very tenderly for a minute or so. " I wanted to see you alone; but how is this, Elsie; have you slept badly? You are not looking half bright enough for a bride, little girl."

" I did so want the sun to shine to-day, Felix," replied Elsie in such a really plaintive, injured tone, that Dr. Paget would have smiled had he not perceived by the tears shining on his foolish little sister's lashes that she really took the matter seriously to heart.

"You did so want the sun to shine?" he repeated, with his eyes still bent thoughtfully and anxiously now upon the pretty, eager face looking up into his own; " but it is very early yet, Elsie. Perhaps by and bye your wish may be accomplished. I hope it will, dear."

" But I don't think there is any chance, Felix;" she persisted with the half sad, half petulant manner of a child accustomed to have everything its own way, and unable to comprehend *why* it should be thwarted. " Those clouds have no signs of breaking in them."

" Yet it is a small matter to be vexed about,

Elsie," said her brother with increasing gravity ; "we all go through life *wanting* the sun to shine upon us, but very few of us get more than occasional glimpses of it. A thoughtful woman poet has quaintly, but truly said, that ' No lot below for one whole day eludeth care,' and I believe she referred especially to the lot of married people. My little sister must try to prepare herself for, at least, the ordinary trials which a wider mixing with and knowledge of the world must inevitably bring her. I am afraid, Elsie, we are all more less guilty of having unfitted you for dark and cloudy days."

"I hate metaphors, Felix," replied Elsie, pouting a little, but holding her brother's hand very affectionately the while ; "and you ought to know that I am not so foolish as to expect unclouded sunshine in the sense you mean. I don't see anything very unnatural in wanting to have had a bright day for my wedding. Everybody does that. I know Edgar will be disappointed too."

Felix did smile very slightly now, but he checked himself immediately, and only remarked—

"I don't think Mr. Carlyon will care two straws about it. You are, or ought to be, enough of sunshine for him, Elsie. But look here, you have nearly made me forget what I promised to give to you."

He took a small morocco case from his pocket as he spoke, and placed it in his sister's hand.

"Oliver did not like you to go away without some little remembrance from him, but he said he was ashamed to offer his mite amidst the costly gifts you have lately been receiving, so he kept it, poor fellow! till this morning, and then asked me to bring it in to you. See, Elsie, it is only a plain gold cross with a very simple little chain to it. I don't know why he chose a cross, as he is not a Roman Catholic; but I think it exceedingly pretty and in admirable taste, and so I told him. You must find an opportunity of thanking him by and bye."

"I like it very much indeed," said Elsie

warmly; " and will certainly wear it for my old friend's sake. I suppose (with a smile that had nothing of fear or doubt in it) James Oliver thinks with you, Felix, that my future life will have plenty of crosses in it, and therefore he has sent me this significant emblem; but anyhow, it was most kind of him to remember me at all, and you may be sure I shall find an opportunity of thanking him —— Oh, Joanna, how you startled me!"

This last observation had reference to Elsie's sudden consciousness of loving arms wound tightly round her waist, and it needed not that she should even turn her head to guess who their owner was —nobody in the house moved about in the same quiet, noiseless way as Joanna.

" I woke up suddenly and missed you, my darling. It was not likely I should spare you one unnecessary moment away from me on this last morning. Have you been out, Elsie?"

"No, but I was going just into the garden when Felix stopped me. Look, Jo, what a nice present Mr. Oliver has sent me. I am sure he need not have been ashamed of its insignificance, —it is quite lovely, and must have cost a great deal of money."

Joanna took it into her hand for a moment, touched it tenderly, almost reverentially (but that might have been for the emblem) and then returned it without a word to Elsie.

" You had better both have a stroll in the garden," said Felix, " the others won't be down for this half hour at least, and you will like to enjoy your woman's talk in quiet. I have to return now to the surgery."

So the sisters went out together and remained walking to and fro in the most sheltered path they could find, till Arthur was sent to call them in to the early breakfast. I have no doubt that Joanna meant on this occasion to give her little sister a great deal of excellent advice, that her conscience had decided that it would be well and proper so to do ; but somehow the talk between them on this last morning never reached the point of exhortation and warning which the elder sister believed afterwards it ought to have done, and she could only console herself by the reflection—which I think was a very wise one—that if her many and constant prayers for Elsie were to be heard, God himself would so order the circumstances of her life as to bring her, through their influence and teaching, safely and surely at last into His own fold.

*　　*　　*　　*　　*

"Perfect, quite perfect!" decided Mrs. Vining, when Elsie, in her really exquisite dress of white lace (a present, as was also the splendid veil, from her father-in-law), came and stood before her mother and elder sister for approval. "Edgar must have your portrait taken in Paris just as you are now. You will really make the most lovely picture ever painted."

"Bless her! so she will," said the mother, who really felt too much to be otherwise than natural to-day. "Where is Mr. Paget, I wonder. Do go and find him, Joanna, and tell him to come and look at Elsie."

Mr. Paget, when found and brought in, quite agreed with the others that the bride was looking faultlessly beautiful, and then Elsie, who had got very red during all these flattering speeches, was kissed and caressed (with a due regard, however, to her elegant attire), again and again by each member of her admiring family, and when at length she was allowed to sit down and be quiet they entertained her and one another by conjectures as to what the bridegroom would think of her, and expressions of their hope that he would not fail at least to esteem himself the very luckiest man in the whole world. Were it possible he could do otherwise, Mrs. Vining remarked (with her usual spirited and strong minded way of viewing things) she should like herself to have the punching of his head, or the grinding of him, bodily, into the very finest powder.

"Why it seems but the other day that poor Lillie was married," observed Mrs. Paget, with a profound sigh (her eldest daughter's speech had no doubt brought Mr. Richard Wilmot to her mind), " and how bright and pretty and happy she looked, you remember. How little we any of us thought what a beast that man would turn out, or what a life of care and anxiety was in store for her. Thank God, Elsie is safe from all that sort of thing, but upon my word marrying one's daughters isn't lively work when it comes to the point. There's only Joanna left now, and I'm really glad to believe she hasn't much chance of going off. These events shatter the nerves so horribly."

" Joanna looks remarkably well to-day," graciously admitted Mrs. Vining, who, conscious of looking resplendent herself in her new silver grey poplin, trimmed with black lace, was in an excellent temper. " I shouldn't be surprised if she did find a husband after all—a curate for instance, who would be thankful for a hard working wife, or a Wesleyan minister, who would admire and approve her severe style of costume, and be edified by her general seriousness. You had better not make too sure of keeping Joanna *ad infinitum*, I think."

"Oh, stuff!" responded Mrs. Paget, not choosing at any time to be contradicted by her widowed daughter. "Joanna would think it a sin to fall in love, and a greater sin to marry without it. What o'clock is it, Mr. Paget? The bridesmaids surely ought to be here."

Two carriages drove to the door as the lady of the house spoke. The first contained the three young ladies who were to act with Joanna as bridesmaids to Elsie, young friends of her own, who thought her, of course, the happiest and most fortunate girl in the universe; the second vehicle belonged to Mrs. Richard Wilmot, who, having left her husband to come on to the house when he pleased, was going to accompany the bridal party to church.

There was not much time for her either to look at Elsie now or to be looked at and admired herself. She could only bestow a hurried but hearty embrace upon her sweet little sister, and whisper to Mrs. Paget that Richard was very respectably "got up," and had promised to behave with the greatest propriety.

Then the carriages for the whole bridal party were announced; Felix and James Oliver waited at the door to hand the ladies in; and away they all drove to seal the fate of as happy and innocent a child as ever took care and trouble to her heart through the medium of a wedding ring.

CHAPTER XVII.

MR. RICHARD'S CONDUCT AT THE WEDDING BREAKFAST.

Owing to some unexpected delay in the vestry after the ceremony, some little difficulty concerning the signature of one of the witnesses, the wedding party did not arrive at Bayswater till quite half an hour later than had been calculated upon.

The guests invited to the breakfast (there were not a great number), had all arrived, and some of them were getting very weary and impatient of this long waiting for the good things they knew had been provided for their entertainment. Mr.

Richard Wilmot at any rate was unmistakeably weary, and unquestionably impatient. He had taken but a frugal meal at home, and that earlier than usual. Lillie had assured him they should sit down to breakfast not later than half-past eleven. It was just a quarter past twelve when the carriages drew up, one after the other, at the door, and Mr. Richard felt and looked like a basely deceived and injured individual.

He had instructed his wife to introduce him as soon as she could to the bridegroom, rightly conjecturing that none of her family would be over zealous in performing that ceremony — so poor Lillie, who had cried a good deal in the church, and was now horribly nervous on the subject of her Dick's possible misdemeanours, seized an opportunity when she saw Mr. Carlyon for a moment disengaged, and, going up to him very timidly, asked if she might introduce her husband.

Edgar, who—as the reader will already have discovered—was not immensely interested in any of the Pagets save his own beautiful Elsie, did not really, for a second or two after Lillie had accosted him, remember who she was. A bridegroom, surrounded by pretty and elegantly dressed young women, most of them strangers to him, may surely be pardoned a little mental obscurity, and Mrs. Richard Wilmot, in white flowing robes, and a most becoming crape bonnet, was quite another person—at any rate in a young man's eyes —from poor Lillie in an old brown dress, indifferently made and untidily put on.

"I am Elsie's sister," she explained with a half smile, observing the bridegroom's perplexity; "my husband, Mr. Wilmot, desires to be introduced to you. I believe you have not met yet."

Edgar, thus enlightened, had no choice but to bow with his Parisian grace, to smile encouragingly upon his really pretty sister-in-law, and to say that he was honored by Mr. Wilmot's request. Then Lillie fetched her tyrant, who was not very far off, and made the gentlemen known to each other, rejoicing unfeignedly that the sudden summons to table at that moment prevented even the briefest conversation between them.

"You have done this on purpose," muttered Mr. Richard, surlily, to his wife, as he followed her into the breakfast room, "but I'll be even with you yet, my lady. That fine gentleman shall not go away before I have had a talk with him, and he has acknowledged me as his brother-in-law."

I need scarcely say that this threat did not tend to raise poor Lillie's spirits, or to render the next hour a more agreeable one to her. Had her life depended on it she could never afterwards have told what healths were drunk, what toasts were given, what speeches were made. Her whole attention was absorbed in watching her husband, her whole mind taken up with the terrible fear that he would expose himself in one way or another, and bring shame and confusion upon them all. Happily, at the beginning of the breakfast, his hunger being a very real thing, and Mr. and Mrs. Paget, with Mrs. Vining as coadjutor, attending to the constant replenishing of his plate, he did not attempt to talk to any one, and the worst that the most vigilant observer could have said of this unwelcome wedding guest would have been that he was a wolf, suffering from a week's starvation; but as soon as the champagne (a favourite beverage of Mr. Richard's) began to circulate freely, there came a noticeable change in that gentleman's whole manner and conduct. He was seated between Joanna Paget and one of the prettiest of the bridesmaids, a gentle, timid girl not yet out of the schoolroom. It was upon this innocent and inexperienced young lady that Mr. Richard's first attacks were destined to be made. His unhappy wife heard him commence the conversation by asking her, in by no means a subdued voice, if she had ever been a bridesmaid before, and if it didn't make her mouth water to be a bride.

"Oh, come now," he said, in a vulgar, bantering tone, "we're not so modest as we want to make out. I know all about it. I'm a married man, my dear—worse luck! when such pretty creatures as you are to be had—and so I'm behind the scenes. All girls want to get husbands after they're fourteen, and I take it you must have passed that verdant age by at least a couple of years. Have some more champagne—a glass with me now—it will do us both good : there's nothing like plenty of champagne at these very slow kind of festivities."

As Mr. Richard beckoned to one of the waiters in attendance to bring the wine, the young lady quietly removed her glass out of her officious neighbour's reach, and looked very much inclined to remove herself also. Hitherto, in spite of Mr. Wilmot's loud voice, nobody except his wife had appeared to notice how he was going on. There was plenty of conversation and some merriment at other parts of the table, and all the Pagets had settled beforehand that they would contrive to talk incessantly and keep everybody else talking, that Mr. Dick's probable vulgarities and excesses might escape observation.

But of course no act, however trivial, of that gentleman's could escape the observation of his poor, watchful wife. While he was tossing off the fresh supply of champagne he had called for, and quizzing, in a very coarse manner, the pretty girl beside him for what he designated her mock modesty, Lillie contrived, by a series of telegraphic signals, to make Joanna understand that she was to endeavour to draw Mr. Richard's attention to herself, and thus rescue his other neighbour from a position which was evidently becoming unendurable to her.

Now Joanna Paget was about the worst person in the world to whom such an appeal could have been made. She had little tact at command, less ready wit, and no small talk of any sort likely to interest her very common-minded and most objectionable brother-in-law. And then, over and above the disapproval and abhorrence of Mr. Richard Wilmot, which she shared in common with all her family, Joanna had that sensitive and especial shrinking from him personally, which quiet, undemonstrative women often feel towards loud-voiced, boisterous men.

Her look now, in answer to poor Lillie's pleading glances, seemed to say—

"What can I do? Don't you know that you are requiring of me an absolute impossibility."

Nevertheless, as Lillie's half tearful and wholly sorrowful eyes continued to plead, Joanna rushed wildly into the breach by touching Mr. Richard (with about as much good will and familiarity as she would have touched a mad bull) on the shoulder, and asking him if he was not going to try some pine apple.

In a moment he had swung his heavy body round, and was confronting, with an odious grin of amusement, his very demure and now frightened-looking sister-in-law.

"Very civil and attentive of you upon my honor, Miss Jo. I really had forgotten, in the interest my bewitching neighbour on my right excited, that there was another fair lady on my left expecting her share of gallantry and manly devotedness. Pine apple did you say, my love? Yes, as much as ever you please of it. I'm uncommonly fond of pine apples raised in English conservatories, but if you ask me whether I care about those tenpenny and eighteenpenny things from the West Indies they sell in the streets, why I tell you, frankly, I would'nt give a bob for a whole peck of them—not but what I have been fool enough before now to buy a threepenny slice off one of those fruit trucks you see about in the summer, lots of them always at Paddington, but they didn't agree with me anyways, Miss Jo, they. didn't, upon my honor. Cheap and nasty, you know, as the old proverb says; at least if it isn't a proverb its something else, which will be all the same a hundred years hence, as I tell my wife there when she complains that I don't quite come up to her—notions—of—a hero—of romance—or in other words—of a fine gentleman!"

The effect of this brilliant and remarkable speech will be the better appreciated when it is explained that long before it was finished, there was a dead silence all round the table. Mr. Richard had succeeded at last in monopolizing the whole attention of every one of his father-in-law's guests. In vain, Mr. and Mrs. Paget, with Felix and Georgina Vining, endeavoured in their shame and disgust to set the listeners talking again, to interest them in something apart from Lillie's husband. Even those who felt for the family, and would gladly have appeared inattentive to what was going on, were compelled by a disagreeable sort of fascination, having once been drawn in as spectators and audience, to maintain those characters to the end of the play. Mr. Richard Wilmot, sober, was very far from a pleasing or attractive individual. Mr. Richard Wilmot, tipsy, combined with his other peculiarities so strong an element of the ludicrous, that it was a most difficult thing for anybody not immediately connected with him to avoid being amused while watching and listening to his absurdities.

Even the elder Mr. Carlyon had for a moment

a merry twinkle in his respectable eye, as his disreputable fellow-guest related to the shrinking Joanna his experience on the subject of cheap pine-apples, and itinerant fruit stalls. But, looking across to his son, he became convinced that his own amusement was by no means shared in that quarter. There was an expression of real and acute pain, as well as of sickening disgust, on the bridegroom's handsome face, and the poor little bride, growing red and pale by turns, was endeavouring in vain to attract his notice, and win him from any further attention to the odious man opposite.

" These people have done wisely," soliloquized Mr. Edgar's papa, " in keeping their entertaining relative in the back ground till now. Had Edgar been favored with his acquaintance a day earlier, I am not at all sure, judging by his expressive countenance at this moment, that I shouldn't have played my long game of patience in vain.'

Before Mrs. Paget could decide or take mute

counsel of her husband as to whether it would be better to carry off the ladies at once, or remain with them upon the chance of their presence being some sort of check on Mr. Dick, that merry and elated gentleman had resumed his pleasant talk with Joanna.

"What, don't my wit enliven you, my dear?" he said, observing that his sister-in-law's face became graver and paler with every word he uttered; "but, oh, dear, I remember now" (and here he winked across the table quite indiscriminately) "you are the pious one of the family—the Moravian saint, the little grey quaker, going about with your basket of tracts, like Red Ridinghood with her—something or other. Only I hope the naughty wolf won't eat you up, my dear—plenty of wolves in sheep's clothing amongst your religious folks, Miss Jo, I can tell you; and they make a great feast when they catch an innocent like you; all in white, too, I declare, and looking dainty and nice enough for the best of them. There's that young fellow opposite to us (I hope he isn't a wolf, though) glaring either at you or at me as if he wanted to eat us right up—he's a doctor, ain't he, Miss Jo?"

But Miss Jo was not at all likely to answer the question. She had endured just as much as her strength of mind and nerves enabled her to do, and on Mr. Richard's sudden allusion to James Oliver, not knowing in the least what would come next, the poor harassed girl, with a great gulp, as if forcing down hysterical sobs, pushed back her chair, and made a rapid escape from the room.

This was the signal for a general movement on the part of the breakfast guests. The master of the house led all those who were not privileged to accompany the bride upstairs into the front drawing-room, and while Felix and James Oliver did their best to entertain the younger ladies, the elder ones sought the easy chairs and couches, and spoke together in whispers of the disgraceful conduct of poor Lillie Wilmot's husband, and the terrible mistake the family had made in having him at the wedding at all.

Mr. Paget, whose wrath had been roused to the utmost, returned the moment he was free to the dining-room, where Mr. Dick had remained alone on the departure of his companions. Startling that gentleman as he was in the midst of replenishing his glass—it was a tumbler this time—from a wine bottle that had only been half emptied, the indignant host thus briefly addressed his guest and son-in-law.

" I have sent for a cab, Richard Wilmot, which is to convey you from my house and my sight for ever. Let no possible circumstances tempt you, as you value your own safety, to venture into my presence, either here or elsewhere, again. And, as my last word to you, let me add that if my daughter had not the misfortune to be your wife, I would have had you kicked by my servants, like a dog, as you are, off these premises to-day."

Now Mr. Richard, far gone as he was, had still enough of his wits left to understand every word of this very unequivocal speech from his justly incensed father-in-law. He stared at him for a moment certainly, with a half vacant, half-cunning look, but then he said, steadily enough, if a little thickly—

"All right, old gentleman! I've had a famous breakfast, and am quite ready to go home and get a comfortable snooze till dinner time. Much obliged for your politeness in sending for a cab; but I say"—for Mr. Paget had already turned, his back upon him—"perhaps it wouldn't be troubling you too much to send word to the lady who has the misfortune to be my wife, that our vehicle has been ordered. You understand me clearly, old fellow! don't you? Where I go, my dutiful Lillie goes, and where adverse circumstances, over which I have no control, forbid my bestowing my society, my dutiful Lillie cannot think of bestowing hers either. Don't let her keep me waiting now—that's all."

Mr. Paget, swelling and boiling over with rage, left his son-in-law's presence, and abruptly sought admittance into that upstair room where the bride, ready dressed for the journey, was standing and weeping bitterly amidst a circle of weepers.

"Oh, by George ! this is too much !" burst spontaneously from the lips of the worried and indignant gentleman, as he advanced towards the closely gathered women ; "what in the name of patience is the good of crying, like so many children, because that has come to pass which you all wanted, and which you all know now to be a piece of monstrous good luck. Elsie, you are a little fool to make yourself look ugly in your new husband's eyes the moment you belong to him, and as for the rest of you, I can only say you deserve flogging , except Lillie, who, indeed, has something, poor girl! to cry and make a noise about."

" And it's for her as much as for Elsie that *we* are crying," spok e out Georgina Vi ning spiritedly, "such a shame and disgrace as that beast has brought upon us all. I hope you've turned him out of the house, sir ?"

" I have sent for a cab to take him away," said Mr. Paget in a milder tone, and drawing poor Lillie a little apart from the others ; " but, my dear," he continued in a low voice to her, " I am sorry to tell you that your husband insists on taking you with him. I am afraid you must yield for this once, but if you will come home to your mother and myself, Lillie, I will arrange everything in a few days, and bind him over to forego altogether his claims upon you."

In his anger against Mr. Richard, and in his deep pity for his hapless daughter, Mr. Paget quite believed at the moment that he should have the power of doing what he promised.

But Lillie, though her eyes were swollen with the tears she had shed as well as with those that were yet to come, and though her face and even her lips were as white as the dress she wore, gave the same answer to her father that she had pre-viously given to her brother.

"I will not leave him, papa; not yet, at any rate. I am not afraid of him; he will never injure me; he never has, and you know I am not often cast down as I have been to-day. Elsie, my love, my darling!" she exclaimed, turning suddenly to her little sister, and fighting desperately with the sobs that were endeavouring to choke her words, "I *must* give you my last kiss, I *must* say good bye to you now."

Mr. Paget was far too great a coward to continue any longer as a looker on in that upstair room. For the glory of manhood at threescore I regret to have to chronicle that he sneaked down again with much less dignity of carriage and stern self-assertion than had distinguished him as he came up. He was at the front door, however, waiting to hand Mrs. Wilmot into her cab. She did not speak another word at that time, and her veil was over her face ; but the father was conscious of a very tender, grateful squeeze from the slight fingers that clung somewhat yearningly round his own ; and, leaving the servants to give

Mr. Dick any assistance he might require, poor Mr. Paget returned in anything but a jovial state of mind to his family and guests in the drawing-room.

A few minutes more and the bride's very handsome travelling carriage, with its four noble horses glittering in their new silver harness, appeared in the place of poor Lillie's humble cab, and attracted a crowd of idlers to the spot.

Then the final adieux were hurried over, the bridegroom giving unmistakeable symptoms of being even nervously anxious to get away. The bride hid her disfigured face as well as she could under her thick travelling veil; her mother and sisters recollecting that all sorts of curious and prying eyes were upon them, kept their sorrow in check; and the father and brother and James Oliver (that true old friend of the family) took leave of Elsie and her husband with grave though composed countenances, and a few whispered words of hope and blessing for the little girl they found it hard at this last moment to lose.

To lose too, in all human probability, for many, many years, for quite an indefinite period indeed, unless they could go to her ; for Georgina Vining testified to having overheard the bridegroom say to his father at the conclusion of a long whispered dialogue between the two :

" Thank Heaven, we are to live out of England ! I would willingly consent never to set foot on my native shores again if the alternative were to meet even once more, on terms of equality, that low, disgusting fellow my wife's sister has made the fatal mistake of bringing into the family."

Happily for Mr. Edgar Carlyon's chance of enjoying his honey-moon, the gift of second sight had not been accorded to him.

CHAPTER XVIII.

THE FEVER IN THE HOUSE.

ELSIE had been gone rather more than a week, and a state of apparently changeless gloom and monotony had settled down on the family at Bayswater. Two or three short letters had reached them from the bride, written at different places where the travellers had halted on their way to Italy, but this was all of the most mildly exciting nature that had occurred since that memorable wedding breakfast at which Mr. Richard Wilmot had so greatly distinguished himself.

Lillie had not been near her old home again, and though both Mrs. Vining and Joanna had called on separate occasions to see her, they had gathered nothing more than that Dick continued sulky and obstinate, and that poor Lillie herself was becoming reckless and indifferent to every- thing. Not a syllable of the Paris plan had she yet breathed to any of her own family. Joanna had insisted on her accepting the money she had previously offered, and with many tears and dismal convictions that she should never be able to repay it, Mrs. Wilmot had kissed and thanked her generous sister, and said with at any rate momentary sincerity—

"Ah, Jo dear, I begin to wish with all my heart that I were more like you, and then I should welcome death as the richest boon that could be bestowed upon me."

This, however, was only an impulsive utter- ance, as Joanna soon discovered when she at- tempted to speak of the consolations of religion to her much tried sister; for then Lillie mani- fested unmistakeable weariness, and in a short time broke in upon the affectionate admonitions of her companion by entreating her, as she went home, to call at the circulating library where she was in the habit of getting her books, at a penny a volume, and ask them to send her round a fresh set without delay.

There was clearly no soil here at present on which the good seed could be sown with any reasonable hope of its springing up, and bringing forth fruit that should withstand both summer's heat and winter's cold. Joanna walked from her sister's house in a state of depression and discouragement that had become but too familiar to her of late, and with her conscience (somewhat a morbid one as I have said before) writing bitterer things than ever against herself for her want of influence, her uselessness, generally, in a spiritual sense, amongst her own family.

To add to the universal gloom which was weighing upon the Pagets at this time, the weather had been, ever since Elsie's departure, and indeed for some days previous, hopelessly dull, cheerless, and uncomfortable. It was not alone the absence of the sun that rendered it so, but a peculiar density and closeness of the atmosphere, in which damp vapours appeared to hang all throughout the day, and to find an entrance even through the most carefully closed doors and windows. It was an especially unhealthy time, and those who did not become absolutely ill felt its influence on their spirits and temper. Mrs. Vining fumed and grumbled terribly from morning till night, quarrelled with her mother, snapped at Arthur, flew into passions with the servants, and made herself otherwise exceedingly obnoxious to those who had the misfortune to live with her. She appeared to think that the weather was an injury and an annoyance inflicted exclusively upon herself, that nobody else had any right to complain of it, that nobody else could by any possibility be suffering from it.

She would have known, and, it is to be hoped, *felt* differently, had she gone out into the highways and byways of that great city and taken even one passing look into the homes of the poverty stricken multitudes, where narrow, close, uncleanly rooms and insufficient food, were just now uniting with the unhealthy state of the atmosphere in bringing that terribly destructive fever to its height, and filling the churchyards with graves, which were principally those of the little ones.

Felix and his partner. had been alarmingly overworked for some time, the former especially, because he believed his own strength to be superior to that of James Oliver, and insisted on sparing his friend all the labour he could. But even he was knocked up at last, and there came a day when he felt himself quite unable to rise in the morning, and had no choice but to take, with as much resignation as he could muster, the repose he had so long stood in need of. He knew that nothing more serious than physical exhaustion ailed him, so he suffered Joanna to become his nurse, and all the family went in and out of his sick room as they pleased.

The one who, with the exception of Joanna,

pleased to be oftenest there was Dr. Paget's little nephew, Arthur. The child had been deprived of his usual exercise of late; his mother was irritable with him; he had no fresh amusements of any kind, and there was a certain degree of novelty attached to his uncle's being laid up in bed, and a considerable degree of comfort in the aspect of the orderly room, with its small, cheerful fire, that interested this young gentleman, and made him esteem it an especial treat to be admitted, with his playthings, into the apartment.

But after the first two or three days the novelty was over, and Joanna began to notice that the child looked languid and weary, that he often threw aside his toys and laid down before the fire half asleep for an hour at a time. She mentioned this to Arthur's mother, and recommended her to let him be oftener in the air, in spite of the weather; but Georgina said peevishly that the damp atmosphere would give him cold, and that she herself spoiled her dresses and got a headache by going out. By and bye the weather *must* change, and then he should be in the air all day.

It was no doubt from the weather not changing, nor showing any disposition to change, that Dr. Paget was kept so long a prisoner. He rebelled in spirit very much against this unpleasant state of things; but Joanna, who really was in her element in a sick room, soothed him into quietness if not into patience, and James Oliver came at least once every day to sit an hour or so with him, and give him news from the outer world. Always on these occasions Joanna silently disappeared, and if Arthur had been there she usually took him with her, considering that doctors' talk would not be very edifying or useful to a child of his age.

One evening, when Mr. Oliver had come into the room unannounced, the aunt had to rouse her nephew from a sound sleep into which he had fallen on the hearthrug, while she had been reading aloud to Felix—

The little fellow awoke with a start, and, lifting his flushed face to the pale one bending over him, he said crossly,

" I don't want to move, auntie. I won't come out for anybody. My head aches, and I am so tired."

" You shall lie down on the sofa in the warm drawing-room," Joanna whispered, coaxingly; " and I will get you a nice cup of sweet coffee. Do come now, dear child."

But the dear child only shook his head, and repeated, with increasing fretfulness, " I can't get up ; I am so tired, and I don't want coffee, because my throat is sore."

James Oliver, who had been speaking to Felix, turned at that moment, and walked up to the fire-place.

" What's the matter here ?" he asked in his kind, cheerful voice, " not rebellious again, surely ? Arthur has been such a good boy lately."

" I'm not a bad boy now," replied the little fellow almost with a moan ; " but aunty Joanna doesn't know how tired I am, nor how my head is aching."

In another instant James Oliver had lifted him up in his strong arms, and placed him very tenderly on his own knee.

" Bring the lamp nearer if you please, Miss Joanna," he said in so grave a tone that Joanna, into whose mind some uneasy feelings had already entered, obeyed him with sudden trembling.

" And now Arthur must open his mouth very wide indeed, as wide as if he was going to swallow the biggest sugar plum he ever saw—that's right; that's very cleverly done. Good little Arthur! How long has your head been aching?"

"All day, nearly—worse since dinner; but I'm so tired I should like to go to bed, and I won't take any nasty physic."

" Well, you shall go to bed at once, and I won't give you any physic to-night. You can't walk by yourself, you say? Then I must see if I can carry you. Aunt Joanna will kindly bring a candle, and we'll soon tuck you up warm and comfortable."

Not a question did Joanna ask, not a word did she speak, until her poor little sick nephew was laid in his bed, and the heavy eyes fast closed upon his soft pillow. Then, to her scarcely breathed enquiry, Mr. Oliver replied in a low voice,—

"Yes; I have every reason to fear so. Go down now, and break it to his mother, so that either she or one of the servants may arrange to sit up with him. He will not sleep long, and he will awake, probably, very fretful, and in greater pain than he has felt yet. He must have some cooling drink throughout the night, and I shall be round the first thing in the morning."

Joanna felt really faint and sick as she listened to these words, kindly and guardedly as they were spoken.

" Break it to his mother!" Could Mr. Oliver at all know or guess what such a task would involve of courage, discretion, self-command, and patience? Joanna knew, and for a minute or so she assured herself that this was just the one duty she was unequal to perform. But the next instant she had shaken off a little of the cowardly dread that possessed her, and her only wish was that the announcement to Mrs. Vining might be delayed.

"I think," she said, looking so pale that Mr. Oliver blamed himself for not having broken the matter to her, "I think *I* might sit up with Arthur, without, for to-night, speaking of this illness to his mother. While there is the shadow of a hope that it may not be what you fear, it seems almost needless (she was going to say 'cruel') to alarm so excessively timid a person as Mrs. Vining."

He heard her quietly to the end of her suggestion, and then answered with that firmness which doctors are obliged to cultivate.

"Miss Joanna, you have quite enough nursing during the day—not to speak of your labours out of the house. I must really exact a promise from you that you husband all your strength for my patient in the other room. With regard to not telling Arthur's mother of his symptoms to-night, believe me it would be a mistaken kindness. I *know* what is the matter with him. He will be much worse to-morrow."

And so, as Joanna Paget, like all such humble, meek-hearted women, found simple obedience much easier than argument or opposition, she left Mr. Oliver at once, going for a few minutes to her own room to gain strength and courage for what she had, at least tacitly, promised to do down stairs.

"How does Felix seem now?" said Mrs. Paget, looking up from her game of cribbage with her husband, as Joanna entered the drawing-room. "That was James Oliver, I suppose, who came in ten minutes ago?"

"Yes," Joanna replied, glancing furtively at Mrs. Vining, who was sitting with her feet on the fender, gazing moodily into the fire, and doing nothing.

"But I asked you how your brother was, first," resumed Mrs. Paget, showing every disposition to quarrel with somebody, "and you answer by a senseless affirmative, without even taking the trouble to look at me as you speak. Has Mr. Oliver turned your head, child?"

"Felix appears better to-night I think," Joanna said now, but still with her thoughts directed towards the one subject. "He had his tea an hour ago, and appeared quite to enjoy it."

"And pray where have you left Arthur?" enquired Georgina, turning lazily, and exhibiting a very ill-tempered face to her sister. "I am sure it can't be good for him to stay so long as he does in that hot room."

"Arthur is in bed," replied Joanna, with so very sinking a heart that her voice trembled a little even in uttering those four words. "He complained of feeling tired, and of having a headache when I wanted to bring him away with me, and then Mr. Oliver came over and looked at him, and—advised that he should go to bed at once. He wished me to come and tell you that the child is —not well, Georgina."

With the exception of the two pauses I have indicated she had got out the whole sentence with tolerable composure and steadiness, although before it was finished Mrs. Vining had started from her chair, and was confronting her sister with a face from which every vestige of its usual rich colouring had departed.

"Jo," she cried, the moment the other's voice had ceased, " don't try to make a fool of me. I will have the truth at once. Is Arthur going to have the fever ?"

For by this time Mrs. Vining knew what it was that had knocked up Dr. Paget, and though she had never confessed it, the dread of that terrible epidemic had been her chief motive for keeping Arthur so much at home, and refraining from going out herself.

"Do for goodness sake speak, Joanna, and speak plainly," exclaimed Mrs. Paget now, observing that her second daughter was for the moment rendered mute by Mrs. Vining's sudden pallor and excitement. "Arthur had nothing the matter with him at his dinner to day."

"Hold your tongue, mother," almost screamed Georgina, clutching wildly at her sister's hands. "I will *make* her speak if you will only be quiet. Jo," (in an abruptly lowered voice that seemed altogether unlike her own), "the truth?"

Very tenderly and pityingly, and with tears half hiding the poor mother's face from her view, Joanna then said:

"Mr. Oliver fears he is sickening for the scarlet fever—he has all the premonitory symptoms, but—"

"Then I shall die!" was Georgina's first impulsive comment, breaking in upon her sister's unfinished sentence, as she threw herself into her chair again with loud and passionate sobs, that because there was the ring of genuine anguish in them thrilled through the hearts of all who had to hear them.

" Oh, do try to quiet her, Joanna," said Mrs. Paget, wringing her own hands, and looking half helplessly, half threateningly at her husband, who had as yet taken no part in the scene, " I don't believe a word of this nonsense ; it's all rubbish, and James Oliver is a noodle to have frightened us for nothing. Mr. Paget, I'm ashamed of you,"--she contined, turning her wrath suddenly upon that astonished and unoffending gentleman —" sitting there with your mouth and eyes wide open, and your daughter crying herself into fits. Why don't you get up like a man and bring Georgina to, and then go and talk to Mr. Oliver about Arthur."

" I know I shall die," Mrs. Vining repeated again, as she rocked herself to and fro on the chair, and threw out her arms as if to forbid any of them to approach her with words of consolation.

" Had you not better go and see your boy, my dear ?" Mr. Paget ventured in his bewilderment to suggest at this point. " If the poor child is suffering he will naturally want his mother, and you will feel happier in comforting and waiting upon him than in crying here and frightening yourself to death, perhaps for nothing."

This was very excellent advice on the part of the old gentleman, and ought to have had the effect of " bringing Georgina to " (whatever that may mean), which his wife had just exhorted him to accomplish. But it did nothing in fact but elicit fresh torrents of tears, and renewed assurances that death to herself would be the inevitable result of her son's having caught the scarlet fever.

Then Mr. Paget, being unacquainted with any other art of " bringing to," went quietly from the room and fetched down Mr. Oliver.

It is astonishing how soon the appearance of one of the male sex, who does not happen to be of kindred blood, will act as a sedative upon the excited nervous system of a woman. The moment this young doctor walked up to Mrs. Vining, withdrew her hands from her face, and held them in a kind, firm grasp within his own, the violence of her sobs abated, and in a few seconds had ceased altogether.

"My dear lady," he said then, "this will never do as a preparation for the grave and important duties you will have to perform as nurse and companion to a dear child, who—forgive me for my boldness in saying it—has been just a little too much spoilt by 'mamma' to make a very patient sufferer. Now cheer up, I entreat of you, and remember that Arthur could not have taken the disease at a better age, and that he is in a position to have every care and comfort that can be bestowed upon him."

Mrs. Vining was quiet now, but her face had still a look both of fear and misery in it which was very distressing to see. She would have asked Mr. Oliver a hundred questions, but that notwithstanding his encouraging words there was something in his manner, or she fancied there was, that made her shrink from the possibility of doubtful or unfavourable answers. One question, however, she could not help asking, I mean that with her nature—by no means a lofty or heroic nature--she could not help it.   This was—

"Will there be much danger of infection to those who nurse and wait upon the child?"

Mr. Oliver did not in the least understand her as referring to herself.   He would have deemed it impossible for a mother who loved her child to have had any personal apprehensions at such a time.   So he answered frankly—

"There is always more or less danger of infection with scarlet fever; young people should especially avoid unnecessary contact with it.   Let the oldest of your servants wait upon you when you are in his room, and keep Miss Joanna away as much as possible.   Now, if you are ready, we will go up together and see how our poor little friend is sleeping, and I will give you full directions for the night."

Whether the mother's heart spoke out at this moment and hushed all selfish fears, or whether Georgina Vining was too cowardly to exhibit her cowardice before Mr. Oliver, we will not pretend to determine. She hesitated only one half minute after he had spoken, and then, with a suddenly flushed face (it had been quite white till now) accompanied him, in silence, to her son's room.

CHAPTER XIX.

A LITTLE SPARK BLOWN OUT.

THERE could scarcely have been found in the whole of London a worse subject for scarlet fever, or indeed for a bad illness of any description, than Arthur Vining. From his very infancy he had been suffered, through a weak mother's unreflecting indulgence, to lead a life that would have tried a child of a much stronger constitution. Late hours, unwholesome and excessive food, irregular exercise, and insufficient mental discipline are not calculated to promote a healthy action of body in any one ; and Arthur Vining, in addition to having been encompassed with all these disadvantages from the time he could run alone, possessed just that kind of feeble, inflammatory constitution which is the least adapted for resisting disease of a serious nature.

Mr. Oliver had, from the beginning, many more fears than hopes concerning the issue of the child's present illness, and though Dr. Paget, who was not even yet well enough to attend personally to his little nephew, did not quite share his friend's apprehensions, he admitted that Arthur was a bad subject, and that it would take some time and trouble to pull him safely through.

Mrs. Vining, after that first night which she had the resolution to spend by her son's bed, made a very tolerable nurse, and indulged in no more hysterics. Her quietness indeed astonished the whole family, and disposed them to sympathize with her even more cordially than they might otherwise have done. Mrs. Paget and Joanna both helped her in her duties, and the latter especially earnestly tried to cheer and comfort her under the anxiety which every day necessarily increased.

But one thing was particularly noticeable, and this was that although the lines in Georgina Vining's face deepened hour by hour, telling of some very powerful and wearing emotions, she would never confess to one particle of doubt as to Arthur's ultimate recovery. Even while he was delirious, and knew none of those around him, she was in the habit of saying that she thought nothing of this as a feature of the illness which could have any connection with its result. Other children, weaker than Arthur, were constantly having the scarlet fever in its worst shape, and as constantly getting well after it. "He *must* get well;" she would sometimes add in almost a defiant tone, and with a sudden gleam in her eye that terrified Joanna, and suggested all kinds of dreadful possibilities in the event of Mr. Oliver's fears about his little patient being realized. For Joanna had been made acquainted with these fears at a very early stage of Arthur's illness, and as she had as yet only dared to hint them, in the vaguest way, to the child's mother, and as the grandmother treated them invariably with contempt (in her case it was genuine incredulity), it was an immense relief to Joanna's mind to be able to speak freely of them either to her brother or James Oliver, and to ask counsel from them as to how, in the event of the worst, they should prepare poor Georgina for it.

Of course, it was not until the delirium was over that any accurate judgment could be formed as to the degree of weakness the fever had left, and which would have to be fought against by every means that science has at command.

The first time the doctor saw the child after that painful stage of the disease had passed, his look told Joanna, who had come into the room with him, that he was at least not more sanguine than he had hitherto been. What it told to the mother—intently watching his features too—it would have been difficult to guess; but as he turned from the bed, after a few kind, cheering words to the child, who lay now so patiently and motionless on it, she caught his hand, and held it tightly in her own strong grasp.

"James Oliver, he is doing well—you are satisfied with the progress he is making—you can assure me now that in a week or two I shall have my boy strong and hearty again?"

There was that strange light in her eye as she spoke which Joanna had so often noticed lately, and Mr. Oliver, though a tolerably brave man, actually quailed and lost a fraction of his healthy colour under it. He could not tell a lie to calm down this fierce woman. Even had he been disposed to prevaricate, Joanna's presence, though she little guessed the fact, would have preserved him from the weakness. He returned Mrs. Vining's searching look with as much composure as he could summon on so brief a notice, and said only—

"I am a cautious doctor, Mrs. Vining. You must wait for my opinion three days longer."

Then she released his hand abruptly, sat down

again by Arthur, and spoke not another word while he remained in the room.

Before those three days expired the fever had returned, had assumed a malignant form, and there was no longer a question in the minds of either Dr. Paget or James Oliver, as to the fatal termination of the malady.

The former, who could just get down stairs now, undertook to announce to Mrs. Vining that all hope was over, and that she must prepare herself to lose her boy.

It was a dreadful task, and Felix felt it to be so; but Mr. Oliver had spoken frankly of his own shrinking from it, and had added that he thought Joanna ought, if possible, to be spared. So Felix, knowing how useless it would be to ask his mother to do it, agreed to see Georgina himself, and to bear alone, at any rate the first shock, of her anguish.

" I wanted to show you a note I have had from poor Lillie," he said, as in obedience to his summons Mrs. Vining came, with her white face, and knees that trembled more than anyone guessed, into the room where her brother waited for her. "How worn out you look, Georgina. Sit down and rest, while you are here, in that easy chair."

"No, I can't sit, Felix. I am not tired. What does Lillie write about?"

"Well, it seems she has heard of our trouble, though we ourselves have kept it so carefully from her, and she writes in her usual impulsive way, and evidently under great excitement, to tell me that although Dick has sworn she shall not come near us, and employed crueller threats than ever to deter her, she is quite resolved on getting to see poor Arthur by stealth—you know how she always doted on the child—and that we may expect her at any minute. Now on all accounts this must be prevented. I shall send her round a decided prohibition at once. Oliver has just told me that the fever is taking a malignant form, and of course you are aware that, under these circumstances, the danger of infection is

much increased. Lillie has never had the disease
at all, and as she could do Arthur no possible
good, it would be very wrong and inexcusable to
expose her to it. My dear Georgina, do sit
down."

This sudden entreaty was suggested to Dr.
Paget by the discovery that his sister was trembling with such violence from head to foot, that
there was really danger of her falling to the
ground if she persisted in trying to stand upright.
But Mrs. Vining did not appear to take in the
sense of what he said. She went near enough to
where he sat to grasp the elbow of his chair,
which formed a support for her, and then, looking into his face with the same gleam in her
eyes which both Mr. Oliver and Joanna had before seen there, she whispered hoarsely—

"Can't fevers be cured when they become
malignant? I *know* they can be cured, Felix."

The voice had changed so abruptly as the
question was succeeded by the defiant assertion,
that Dr. Paget was for the moment at a loss how

to continue his painful task—how to deal with this almost insane woman at his side.

" I am afraid Arthur can't be cured, Georgina," he answered at length in really faltering accents, and without the immediate courage to look up at his sister as he spoke.

But as a dead silence followed these words, he had no choice but to raise his eyes presently and judge of the effect of the terrible announcement he had made.

Mrs. Vining had heard the truth spoken out in plain, audible, unmistakeable words at last. All her passionate resolves to misunderstand the warnings she had hitherto received, to be deaf to the whispers of her own judgment, to defy even Providence itself to inflict this bitter woe upon her, were over now, could never be renewed in her experience.

Whatever the dread extent of the calamity whose shadow was advancing rapidly upon her, whatever its consequences to herself, there was no longer any possibility of evading it, any loophole for the terrified spirit to creep through and escape. There it was, this new and strange and evil thing, and unless she should be smitten with sudden blindness of the mind, it was there to be looked at, and recognized, and accepted, as a solemn and unalterable fact.

Dr. Paget had been quite prepared for a scene of violence, for hysterical tears and rebellious exclamations, for something which should perhaps call for the assistance of the whole family, and might end in the complete physical exhaustion of the undisciplined woman to whom so severe a trial had been sent. But he was not at all prepared for what actually took place.

Georgina Vining's vulnerable part had been reached—through the very centre of her heart the barbed arrow had entered; and neither crying nor loud demonstration of any kind can express, even when the feeblest natures are in question, that suffering into which every faculty of the soul is called to play a part.

So, on hearing Dr. Paget's fiat concerning her

boy, she only retreated slowly to the chair her brother had previously asked her to occupy, and, covering her face with both her shaking hands, remained thus for the space of about ten minutes.

Felix was too weak to rise and go to her, or even to reach the bell which was at some distance from him. He let her be for the time above mentioned; and then, observing that the trembling of her whole body increased, he grew alarmed, and addressed her soothingly and pityingly by name.

No answer was returned to him. She had evidently not heard him call.

"Georgina," he said again in a louder voice, though certainly not a steadier one. "I am afraid I have broken the truth too abruptly to you, after all. My dear sister, my poor girl, I meant to do it gently—but you would not understand—you would not believe."

Then she allowed her hands to drop and revealed a face so piteous in its utter hopelessness, so scared and wan, that Felix was haunted by it for many an after day.

"Oh, but I did;" she said, in a tone that was much too calm to be natural or encouraging. "I did believe, Felix, all the time I seemed to doubt. Thank you for speaking the truth boldly. I know how hard it was to speak it to me. I will only ask you now how long I may expect to keep my boy with me, and then I will go back to him."

Felix in reply to this said frankly he did not know—he had not seen Arthur himself, but he meant to see him by and bye. Mr. Oliver was going to send round a nurse. He hoped his sister would now spare herself all the fatigue she could. Joanna would be forbidden the room entirely.

Before another night had passed—a night of cruel suffering to the poor little dying boy—Mrs. Vining had to be carried fainting to her own bed, from which she rose no more (being happily unconscious of all that was going on) until another grave had been dug and filled in a neighbouring churchyard.

But Arthur, who was quite free from fever or delirium during the last few days of his life, missed his mother, and fretted piteously after her. Joanna discovered this and insisted on being re-admitted to his room. She said she had no personal fears of sufficient weight to deter her from so obvious a duty, and though both Felix and his partner opposed the measure strongly, this quiet, undemonstrative girl gained her point; and sending the hired nurse to wait on Mrs. Vining (whose malady was a sudden clouding of the overwrought brain), she took her station by Arthur's bed-side, and cordially seconded by James Oliver—that unwearying friend of the family—devoted herself, heart and soul, to the teaching, cheering, and supporting of the little footsore pilgrim, as he came in sight of the dark river he was to pass through alone.

Joanna, with all her self-distrust, with all her

tormenting consciousness, of being like Israel's "empty vine," could henceforth indulge a timid hope of having at length been used as a staff for something weaker, frailer, more helpless altogether than herself, to lean against.

Arthur's wayward, rebellious spirit had seemed to be burnt out of him with the fever which had consumed his poor little life also. He was very gentle, very patient during those last few days of his earthly suffering. He told Mr. Oliver he loved him and Auntie Jo so dearly now, and that he should be always looking out for their coming to him in Heaven. "Bring mamma too —poor mamma!" were almost the latest coherent words he ever uttered; and then the tired eyes closed to open no more upon the world of sin and sorrow, from which he had so early been delivered.

It was while the family were in the midst of their first days of mourning for little Arthur, and before his unhappy mother had sufficiently recovered her reason to understand that she was childless—it was in the very midst of this great sorrow and anxiety that poor Lillie came one day abruptly upon them, and announced, with sobs that were nearly choking her, that she had been sent by her tyrant to wish them all good bye.

The Paris scheme had ripened; the necessary funds for removal had somehow been raised; Mr. Richard was in the highest spirits, and they were to start the following week.

It was an especially painful visit—this parting one of poor Lillie's—to all of them. Again she was kindly and warmly, if imprudently, urged to leave her husband and return to her former home. Again she told them that she could never have an easy moment if she deserted him in his down-ward road. She was not fretting about herself, she declared, but at the thought that little Arthur had died without her seeing him, at the miserable aspect of the whole house, and at poor Georgina's critical state both of mind and body.

" Such a time to leave you all!" she moaned, as Felix and Joanna caressed and tried to soothe her, "and not knowing that we shall ever meet again. Oh, indeed, I don't care what becomes of me over there, but it is hard and cruel to be torn away from my own people when they are in such trouble."

They all felt it to be very hard and cruel to lose her, especially under the circumstances which some of them at least guessed were tempting Mr. Wilmot to go abroad. Lillie could derive no consolation from being near Elsie, since this near neighbourhood must bring into collision their strangely antagonistic husbands also.

"There will be awful work, I fear, when those two men meet, and Dick asserts his relationship;" s aid Felix, some time later, in speaking of the matter to his father. And then there came suddenly to his memory the strange dream he had once dreamt of seeing Lillie and Elsie pursued by some dark and alarming object, which, in the end, took the uncomely shape of Richard Wilmot.

CHAPTER XX.

COMING HOME.

It is cheering to turn from gloomy skies and sorrowing hearts, from scenes of sadness and desolation, such as have recently been described, to a bright and joyous spring morning, in the charming, sunny, fascinating, care dispelling city of Paris.

Mr. and Mrs. Edgar Carlyon, having spent a longer time than they originally intended, the whole winter indeed, and even the first chilly months of spring, in basking under the warm, fair skies of Southern Italy, have just arrived in the French capital, and taken possession of the elegant and luxurious home which during their absence has been prepared for them. It is not a very large house that has been chosen for the young couple, ·for neither Elsie nor her husband have any fancy for mere outward display; but it is as perfect otherwise, both in itself and in all its internal arrangements and decorations, as such wealth as theirs, united to a cultivated and perfect taste, could render it. Mr. Carlyon the elder, had taken especial pleasure, during the whole winter, in planning, purchasing, superintending, and, in short, devoting himself generally to labours in connection with this really fairy-like home, to which he was to welcome his son and daughter-in-law. He was as fidgetty and anxious for their arrival, when all was ready, as a schoolboy for his holidays, and thought every day a week while their return was delayed. Elsie's delight and admiration and childish joy, however, when at last they came, quite reconciled him to the long waiting, while it strengthened his conviction that he had secured, by his very clever management, the best and most charming of wives for his only son.

That they were as happy as a strong mutual attachment and the possession of every external accessory to enjoyment could make them, Mr. Carlyon was not slow to discover. He spent the first evening of their arrival with them, listened complacently to all their travelling adventures— Elsie being the chief narrator,—assured himself that Edgar, though less demonstrative than his wife, was really quite satisfied with his new home, and returned to his own bachelor apartment at eleven o'clock, in a very pleasing and comfortable frame of mind indeed.

He had made an appointment with his son for the next morning, apologizing to Elsie for so soon taking her husband away from her; but he wanted Edgar to assist him in choosing a piano (the only thing yet lacking amongst the costly furniture of their house), and which was to be his own gift to his fair daughter-in-law.

The morning has come, a bright, radiant, spring

morning, as I have said at the commencement of this chapter; and Edgar, having kissed his little wife, and told her not to be dull in his absence, has gone to keep his appointment with Mr. Carlyon, and perhaps (for the best of men are but mortal, and given to love change of any kind) to congratulate himself that the honeymoon is over, and with ·it the necessity for exclusive devotedness to feminine society. .

Elsie, of course—loving little simpleton as she is,—feels quite melancholy for at least a quarter of an hour after she is left alone; but suddenly remembering that there is a garden yet to make acquaintance with—a small garden such as French villas in the neighbourhood of the Champs Elysées usually stand in—also that Hector, who has been taken care of by Mr. Carlyon in her absence, is somewhere down stairs, she jumps up in recovered spirits, rings for her hat, and, in a few minutes, is racing with her old favourite, in very unmatronlike fashion, across the miniature lawn, and round the stifly bordered gravel paths, that are shadowed by a small wilderness of linden and acacia trees at the end farthest from the house. There are not many flowers in bloom in Elsie's garden at present, but it is filled with roots and plants of the rarest kind, which promise great things by and bye. And in a warm, sheltered corner, she finds nearly a dozen beautiful white violets, smelling more sweetly, she is perfectly certain, than any violets have ever smelt before; and these she gathers delightedly, and ties into a little bunch, to stick in Edgar's button-hole as soon as he comes home.

After this, as the sun is growing very hot, Elsie sits down on a pretty rustic bench, placed under a curiously twisted pink hawthorn tree on the lawn, and calling Hector to stretch himself in his old lazy fashion at her feet, she begins to feel a little sad in thinking of her former home in England, and of the sorrows that have befallen those she left there in the past six months.

As lightly as possible, however, Elsie's loving correspondents have touched on these domestic afflictions to her. It seemed so hard that the first bright weeks of her married life should be broken in upon by details of suffering, anxiety, and death. They could not, of course, conceal from her that little Arthur had been taken from them—Elsie was in mourning for him still—but though they mentioned Mrs. Vining's illness they never told how long and serious that illness had been, nor for how weary and anxious a time they had feared that the mind of the stricken mother would remain under a perpetual cloud. And there was yet another thing concerning which Elsie had been hitherto left, from motives of kindness, in complete ignorance, and this was the removal of the Wilmots to Paris. She had often wondered, during her sojourn in Italy, that so little was ever said of poor Lillie in any of the home letters she received. She had even thought it unkind of Lillie herself not to write to her; but in reply to some remark to this effect she had once made in a letter to Joanna, the latter had said—"don't judge dear Lillie, for being so poor a correspondent. You know how few pleasant things she ever has to tell us of herself, and how unwilling she is to sadden us by dwelling on her unhappiness. Be assured, Elsie darling, that she neither forgets you, nor feels indifferent to your welfare. We hear that Richard is working steadily just now."

And with this scant intelligence concerning the sister she so dearly loved and tenderly pitied, Elsie had been obliged to content herself. It was some weeks since she had had a letter from home at all, and in these first hours of solitude to which she had been yet condemned since her marriage, it was natural that her thoughts should revert somewhat mournfully, to the days and to the associations from which her married life had already completely severed her.

Perhaps Hector had assisted in bringing up old times and old faces before the mental vision of his young and happy mistress. She could scarcely look at his familiar, though graceless form, without thinking of Felix and Joanna, and

Mrs. Vining, and her father and mother—even of James Oliver, who she knew now had loved the dog for her sake, and would have begged it for his own property had not Mr. Carlyon, her husband, decided that she should not be parted from so old and faithful a friend.

Well, well, all these reminiscences of the past, all this conjuring up of times and persons to which Elsie now first realized that she no longer in any sense appertained, was a natural exercise of the mind on such a lovely, dreamy, spring morning. She might have indulged in it for another hour, sitting under the arching thorn tree, and basking in that pleasant sunshine, had not the appearance of a man-servant coming from the house with letters in his hand, roused her from reverie to action.

" Hi, Hector!" called Elsie, tattooing with her little foot on the back of her sleeping favorite till he awoke with a growl—" hi, good dog — fetch letters to mistress."

And after one of his inevitable fits of yawning

and stretching, Hector condescended to understand the order, and to bound off in the direction Elsie indicated, to receive the letters she waited for.

"Thank you, dear old Hector. And now you may lie down and go to sleep again, for you have brought me something that will interest me far too much to give you any chance of further notice this morning. Don't frisk, you stupid old dog, as if you knew it was an English letter; lie down, and let me enjoy my treasure in peace."

This was Mrs. Edgar Carlyon's treasure.

"My Darling Elsie,—

"I intend this letter to meet you on your arrival in Paris, to be one of the first welcomes you will receive to your new abode— speaking to you, as I am sure it will, of all those who so fondly love you, and who so very earnestly desire that a perpetual blessing may rest on the home over which you will henceforth preside as mistress. I wish I could be with you,

Elsie, as you begin the serious, earnest duties of your life, as you set yourself the task of ruling your household, and ministering in every legimate way to your husband's comfort and happiness. You were such a child, my darling, when you left us that I can scarcely realize the fact that a woman's life of duty, of temptation, and of trial has actually commenced for you, for the little sister whose playthings I stumbled upon only the other day, and who but a short time ago—oh! how short it seems, Elsie !—was laid upon a sick bed from which we had scarcely a ray of hope ever to see her rise. My darling, life and destiny have wonderfully changed for you—the outward gloom and barrenness have all disappeared, and in their stead have come sunshine and fertility, and the promise at least, of a rich and abundant harvest of human joy and blessedness. You rejoice at this, my Elsie, naturally and instinctively rejoice, and we, who care for you so much, rejoice also, and pray that all may be well now and hereafter. I do verily believe that amongst the children of earth there are a few to whom the Father of all grants a very large measure of earthly enjoyment—grants it in love, and so grants it and holds it for them that it shall be neither a snare nor an hindrance, but rather a help to them in their journey to the Heavenly city. Now, my Elsie, I dare not say that you are one of these. When the rule (of happiness being dangerous), embraces so large a proportion of the human family, I have no reason to expect even, that you will be amongst the rare exceptions. I can only say that with my whole heart and soul I wish it might be so; that my darling might be suffered to keep her present joys and yet be led safely and surely onwards to those which are so immeasurably fuller, richer, and sweeter.

" Elsie, should it be otherwise—I mean, should you have to encounter the 'much tribulation,' which, after all, is the appointed road to Heaven, be not dismayed nor discouraged, my darling. You will have strength in the battle you would never have had out of it, and comforts and consolations, if you seek them rightly, that are known only to those who ' suffer in the flesh.' My sermon is done, Elsie; and now we will begin the home gossip.

" Since I wrote last no important changes have taken place here. Georgina's uncertain health and continued shrinking from society, keep our house very quiet indeed, too quiet, I am afraid, to please mamma, whose spirits are very bad, and who says frequently she cannot endure the dulness by which we are surrounded. If it were not for James Oliver we should be left wholly to ourselves, and I don't believe he would come so much as he does if it were not for the comfort his visits so manifestly bring to Georgina. Since Arthur's death she has clung to this kind friend and to me—I suppose, because we were so much with the dear child at the last—in a most extraordinary manner. It seems so strange, Elsie, that Georgina should have come to look upon me as something necessary and soothing to her. I am not surprised that she should derive comfort

and pleasure from Mr. Oliver's society—that is
very natural, for you cannot think how gentle
and tender he is towards her in her affliction—
but that I should be acknowledged as a support
of the most feeble kind to a sister who has hitherto
regarded me as a half crazy fanatic, if not a hypo-
crite, is, indeed, wonderful, and excites my constant thankfulness. You will not be surprised,
Elsie, remembering my old self-accusings, to
hear that I am happier in my own mind than I
have been since my happy schooldays. It is so
good to feel that we are not altogether useless to
those around us. Outwardly, however, I must
confess to two or three sources of anxiety—one is
the apprehension that papa has something which
he keeps to himself, troubling him particularly,
and making him very irritable with mamma,
Georgina, and all of us. I suppose it relates to
business, but as we have been living so quietly
for a long time, and in several ways our home
expenses have diminished, I cannot think that
he is in any great money difficulty. Another of

my anxieties relates to Felix and the gloom and discontent which seem day by day to be growing upon him; and the third and last, my Elsie, is connected, indirectly at any rate, with you and Mr. Carlyon, and involves a little family secret which we have judged it well hitherto to keep from you.

"What will you say, or rather feel, when I tell you that Lillie and her husband are actually living in Paris, not very far from your own quarter of the city. Richard heard of a situation (I believe in a wine merchant's business), and accepted it soon after your marriage. At present he is both working and behaving steadily; but, Elsie darling, we feared to mar the brightness of your honeymoon by telling you this news before. We remembered Mr. Carlyon's disgust at that unfortunate breakfast, and we thought he would be annoyed and perhaps indignant at the idea of finding so uncongenial a brother-in-law settled close to him on his return home. Now that you are in Paris, the fact can no longer be concealed, and indeed we are becoming anxious to know something more of poor Lillie and her surroundings than her own letters are likely to tell us. I enclose you her address, as I am sure she will not venture to come to you, until you either write or go to her. She was most strongly opposed to Richard's acceptance of the situation, and is terribly apprehensive that you may ultimately suffer through their near neighbourhood; but as the thing is done, and Mr. Wilmot is not a man to be advised or dictated to, we must just hope for the best. I am already late for the post, my darling, and can only add now the united fondest love of the entire home circle.

"Ever your affectionate and loving sister,

"JOANNA."

When Elsie raised her eyes on coming to the last word of this long letter, her face, which had flushed deeply as she read Joanna's concluding piece of news, had grown very pale indeed.

Seldom, perhaps, had her mind and heart been divided by such opposing emotions as those which at present filled them. To see Lillie again so soon, to have her living near her, to know that they might meet daily, would have been joy unspeakable had not the hateful form of Dick Wilmot, standing in the back ground, cast a dark and threatening shadow over this otherwise sunny picture. It may be that Elsie had learned more of her own husband's nature during the close communion of the last six months, than she had even guessed at before. It may be that she had some new and peculiar reason to dread his being brought into contact with Richard Wilmot. Anyhow, it was quite plain that the English letter she had so longed for, and so very gladly received, was agitating her in no ordinary degree.

Hector, who had not gone to sleep again at his mistress's bidding this time, seemed to divine that something was wrong, for after standing for a few minutes gazing fixedly at her, through his lazy, half-closed eyes, he suddenly lifted one of his great paws and volunteered to shake hands, by way no doubt of expressing sympathy with the trouble his instinct enabled him to guess.

"Don't tease, Hector!" said Elsie a little crossly, as she gave the offered paw a somewhat rough squeeze, and then put it from her—"I want to think quietly, and not to be worried."

Poor little girl! Just in the same tone, and with the same sort of feeling dictating it, she had said she wanted the sun to shine on her wedding morning. Truly she was one of those who seemed so formed to live in the sunshine that it would become a matter of curious speculation as to how she would ever endure the shade.

Drawing her large hat now completely over her face, Elsie leant back in the corner of her bench, and proceeded to the task of meditating gravely upon the very serious matter which had been brought by Joanna's letter before her notice.

When she looked up again at length, having caught the sound of footsteps coming near her, it was to meet the smiling, loving face of her husband, who bent over her, holding a bouquet—of such flowers as only the Paris markets can produce—in his hand.

END OF VOL. I.

T. C. Newby, 30, Welbeck Street, Cavendish Square, London.

BEDSTEADS, BEDDING, AND BED ROOM FURNITURE.

HEAL & SON'S

Show Rooms contain a large assortment of Brass Bedsteads, suitable both for home use and for Tropical Climates.

Handsome Iron Bedsteads, with Brass Mountings, and elegantly Japanned.

Plain Iron Bedsteads for Servants.

Every description of Woodstead, in Mahogany, Birch, and Walnut Tree Woods, Polished Deal and Japanned, all fitted with Bedding and Furnitures complete.

Also, every description of Bed Room Furniture, consisting of Wardrobes, Chests of Drawers, Washstands, Tables, Chairs, Sofas, Couches, and every article for the complete furnishing of a Bed Room.

AN

ILLUSTRATED CATALOGUE,

Containing Designs and Prices of 150 articles of Bed Room Furniture, as well as of 100 Bedsteads, and Prices of every description of Bedding

Sent Free by Post.

HEAL & SON,

BEDSTEAD, BEDDING,

AND

BED ROOM FURNITURE MANUFACTURERS,

196, TOTTENHAM COURT ROAD,

LONDON. W.

J. W. BENSON,

WATCH AND CLOCK MAKER, BY WARRANT OF APPOINTMENT, TO
H.R.H. THE PRINCE OF WALES,

Maker of the Great Clock for the Exhibition, 1862, and of the Chronograph Dial, by which was timed "The Derby" of 1862, 1863, and 1864 Prize Medallist, Class XXXIII., and Honourable Mention, Class XV, begs respectfully to invite the attention of the nobility, gentry, and public to his establishment at

33 & 34, LUDGATE HILL,

Which, having recently been increased in size by the incorporation of the two houses in the rear, is now the most extensive and richly stocked in London. In

THE WATCH DEPARTMENT

Will be found every description of Pocket Horological Machine, from the most expensive instruments of precision to the working man's substantial time-keeper. The stock comprises Watches, with every kind of case, gold and silver, plain, engine-turned, engraved, enamelled, chased, and jewelled, and with dials of enamel, silver, or gold, either neatly ornamented or richly embellished.

BENSON'S WATCHES.

"The movements are of the finest quality which the art of horology is at present capable of producing."—*Illustrated London News* 8th Nov., 1862.
33 & 34, Ludgate Hill, London.

BENSON'S WATCHES.

Adapted for every class, climate, and country. Wholesale and retail from 20 guineas to 2½ guineas each.
33 & 34, Ludgate Hill, London

BENSON'S WATCHES.

Chronometer, duplex, lever, horizontal, repeating, centre seconds, keyless, astronomical, reversible, chronograph, blind men's, Indian, presentation, and railway, to suit all classes.
33 & 34, Ludgate Hill, London.

BENSON'S WATCHES.

London-made levers, gold from £10 10s., silver from £5 5s.
33 & 34, Ludgate Hill, London.

BENSON'S WATCHES.

Swiss watches of guaranteed quality, gold from £5 5s; silver from £2 12s. 6d.
33 & 34, Ludgate Hill, London.

Benson's Exact Watch.

Gold from £30; silver from £14.
33 & 34, Ludgate Hill, London.

Benson's Indian Watch.

Gold, £23; silver, £11 11s.
33 & 34, Ludgate Hill, London.

BENSON'S CLOCKS.

"The clocks and watches were objects of great attraction, and well repaid the trouble of an inspection."—*Illustrated London News*, 8th November, 1862.
33 & 34, Ludgate Hill, London.

BENSON'S CLOCKS.

Suitable for the dining and drawing rooms, library, bedroom, hall, staircase, bracket, carriage, skeleton, chime, musical, night, astronomical, regulator, shop, warehouse, office, counting house, &c.,
33 & 34, Ludgate Hill, London.

BENSON'S CLOCKS.

Drawing room clocks, richly gilt, and ornamented with fine enamels from the imperial manufactories of Sèvres, from £4 to £7 7s.
33 & 34, Ludgate Hill, London.

BENSON'S CLOCKS,

For the dining room, in every shape, style, and variety of bronze—red, green, copper, Florentine, &c. A thousand can be selected from, from 100 guineas to 2 guineas.
33 & 34, Ludgate Hill, London.

BENSON'S CLOCKS,

In the following marbles:—Black, rouge antique, Sienne, d'Egypte, rouge vert, malachite, white, rosée, serpentine, Brocatelle, porphyry, green, griotte, d'Ecosse, alabaster, lapis lazuli, Algerian onyx, Californian.
33 & 34, Ludgate Hill, London.

THE HOUSE-CLOCK DEPARTMENT,

For whose more convenient accommodation J. W. Benson has opened spacious show rooms at Ludgate Hill, will be found to contain the largest and most varied stock of Clocks of every description, in gilt, bronze, marbles, porcelain, and woods of the choicest kinds.

In this department is also included a very fine collection of
BRONZES D'ART,

BENSON'S ILLUSTRATED PAMPHLET, free by post for three stamps, contains a short history of Horology, with prices and patterns of every description of watch and clock, and enables those who live in any part of the world to select a watch, and have it sent safe by post.

33 & 34, LUDGATE HILL, E.C.

THE TEETH AND BREATH.

How often do we find the human face divine disfigured by neglecting the chiefest of its ornaments, and the breath made disagreeable to companions by non-attention to the Teeth! Though perfect in their structure and composition, to keep them in a pure and healthy state requires some little trouble; and if those who are blessed with well-formed teeth knew how soon decay steals into the mouth, making unsightly what otherwise are delightful to admire, and designating unhealthiness by the impurity of the breath; they would spare no expense to chase away these fatal blemishes. But although most ladies are careful, and even particular in these delicate matters, yet few are sufficiently aware of the imperative necessity of avoiding all noxious and mineral substances of an acrid nature, and of which the greater part of the cheap tooth-powders and pastes of the present day are composed. It is highly satisfactory to point out Messrs. ROWLANDS' ODONTO, or Pearl Dentifrice, as a preparation free from all injurious elements, and eminently calculated to embellish and preserve the dental structure, to impart a grateful fragrance to the breath, and to embellish and perpetuate the graces of the mouth,—*Court Journal.*

ROWLANDS' ODONTO

Is a White Powder, compounded of the choicest and most recherché ingredients of the oriental herbal, of inestimable value in preserving and beautifying the teeth, strengthening the gums, and in giving a pleasing fragrance to the breath. Price 2s. 9d. per box.—Sold by Chemists and Perfumers.

*** Ask for "ROWLANDS' ODONTO."

May be had of every Bookseller.

In 1 Vol. Price 7s. 6d.

PRINCE HASSAN'S CARPET.

BY HOPE LUTTREL.

In 1 Vol. 10s. 6d.

NELLY MILES.

A NOVEL.